INHERITANCE

SANDRA GOLDBACHER

Typeset The Pixelpusher Ltd

Although based on historical research, the main
characters and events are works of fiction.

First published in Great Britain in 2012
by Daughters of History Ltd. Reg. No.7057626
207 Regent Street, 3rd Floor
London W1B 3HH
United Kingdom

www.AGirlForAllTime.com

For my mother, Fiona

After the gong

Amelia Elliot was halfway down the staircase to the school dining room when her life changed forever.

The dinner gong had sounded twice and she was going to be late. She would always think of her life now as 'before the gong' and 'after the gong'. Before the gong, everything had been safe and normal: slightly dull, slightly sad, but safe. She was worried about her Latin exam, she missed her father, she hated Perdita Mildbrace. After the gong, nothing would be safe or normal ever again.

Halfway down the stairs she had stopped running, spotting Miss Lancer looking up at her. Running was forbidden, of course, but The Lance's face was twisted into a tight bud of a smile and Amelia's heart contracted. She was guided into Miss Mapthorpe's study to receive the news. Her mouth went dry.

When she saw the headmistress' face she knew this wasn't going to be a lecture about running in the corridors. Catastrophe hung in the air like ripe fruit.

It was her father: Fear ran through her head. Sluiced through her bloodstream. The old fear, the worst fear. The nightmare she'd had since infancy.

She fixed her eyes on Miss Mapthorpe's mouth: "Ship lost at sea…Sunk without trace…Missing, feared drowned." She'd

almost rehearsed this scene in her head as a way to propitiate God and ward off calamity, but now it was
actually happening.

Amelia said nothing. The room softened to syrup around her. She came to on the Turkey carpet, roused by The Lance's smelling salts and was taken to the sanatorium.

So Amelia didn't need to worry about her Latin exam, or her feud with Perdita Mildbrace. School was over for her. Her Aunt Cora and Uncle Enoch, two complete strangers, would be arriving to take her away. Away from school. Away to their house in London. She was twelve years old and had become that staple figure of storybook openings - an orphan.

Amelia packed her school trunk with the silver-framed photograph of her dead mother and missing-feared-drowned father, covered her pet canary, Miss Lovington's, cage and waited in a window seat for her uncle and aunt to arrive. Waited, lost and frozen-headed as a porcelain doll.

Through the thick glass of the window she saw them step out of their carriage in the drizzling rain. Uncle Enoch was a gaunt, black-clad figure – so tall, with his dark umbrella, that he seemed to blot out the grey sky. He looked entirely unlike his estranged brother Norton - her kind, beloved father. She'd hoped there might be at least some resemblance. On his arm teetered his tiny wife, frills of lilac lace foaming around her throat.

Aunt Cora had an eager, beseeching expression and ardently-parted pink lips. She clutched Amelia to her small, perfumed bosom.

"You poor, pretty, creature. We are going to love you so much. Love you…like our own. And we'll have so much amusement together. We'll get rid of this horrid, plain school dress and you won't have to worry about anything nasty ever again."

Aunt Cora stroked Amelia's plaits. Amelia wanted to snarl and bite her hand. To sink her teeth into the white palm, like a rabid dog, until it streamed with blood, but she curtseyed and lowered her eyes.

"Thank you, Aunt Cora."

Miss Lancer, sensible sober Miss Lancer, clasped her hand and gave her a parcel of books.

"You have a fine brain, Amelia. Don't forget that. We are all alone really, you know. But one can make a good life using one's education. Exercise that brain. With a book you are never lonely. With education you have a solid sense of self-worth."

Aunt Cora laughed nervously and eyed the drab schoolteacher with veiled dread. What could this plain spinster possibly have that anyone could value? But Amelia thanked Miss Lancer and cradled the books gratefully.

Her classmates peered through the carriage window as

she drew away. Amelia hid her face from their pity and
excitement at the drama, breathing back tears, expressionless.
She chanted inside her head, *"Missing- feared-drowned does
not mean dead. Missing-feared-drowned does not
mean dead."*

Her heart was a flint pebble as she left school behind. The
solid Georgian building, which had loomed so large in her
life, shrank now to a tiny doll's house as the carriage cleared
the driveway and rumbled on towards London.

 If she held her breath for long enough, could she die?

Uncle

Uncle Enoch and Aunt Cora's house was tall and ornate and pilastered and sat on a smart, stuccoed London crescent overlooking Regent's Park.

A young parlourmaid, with an open, shining face, like an apple, answered the door. She eyed Amelia with interest as the pasty-faced hall-boy hauled her luggage upstairs.

Amelia was to follow Aunt Cora to the parlour to have tea. She clutched Miss Lovington's cage to her chest. The room was filled with a heavy scent of tuberoses. It was dizzyingly full of objects. Every surface was polished like toffee and crammed with ornaments: Plaster spaniels, stuffed humming-birds under glass domes, bowls of waxen fruit, dancing figurines.

Amelia felt trapped. The green silk wallpaper swam with trails of lilies and pansies. Even the windows were layered with glass cases filled with plant tendrils. Light filtered greenly into the room, as though it were underwater. It was hot and moist like the palm house at Kew Gardens, which she'd visited with school. Sweat began to pool in the armpits of her tight, school-dress.

Aunt Cora beamed, "I see you're admiring my pretty treasures! I think you're like me, Amelia. Oh, how I long to fill your life with prettiness, so you won't have time to think of ugly, bad, sad things."

Amelia wanted to spread her arms and stamp and whirl and bring the twee gewgaws crashing to the ground in an eruption of painted china and glass.

Aunt Cora patted the spindly pink silk sofa for Amelia to sit beside her.

"Soon, I hope, you'll come to think of me as your new mama. The mama you never truly had. And you can put away those dull old books that frightful frump gave you! Latin and science. Ghastly! We'll dress you adorably and arrange your beautiful hair."

Aunt Cora put her hand up to stroke one of Amelia's plaits again and Amelia flinched. Aunt Cora withdrew her hand.

"But I like books... and learning," Amelia said.

Cora laughed, "Well of course one does. I have all the new novels. And art...makes one's life so pleasant. You have so many new things to learn so you may fit in to the London Season..."

Amelia stared at her, surly and numb.

"...dancing of course, embroidery...and, oh my dear - the latest thing – painting on porcelain! We shall paint our very own adorable teacups!" Cora trilled on and on and Amelia felt her head swim.

She paused to draw breath, "Now…do you think you might like to start calling me mama?"

Amelia's face set like a mask.

"Well…maybe, in time. Oh, my sweet, it's just that, you remind me so much of…someone"

"My mother?" said Amelia, hopefully.

"No dear. I only met her once…at the wedding. A very simple affair – not inelegant, but not quite…quite. She had lovely hands. Now what say you to some new clothes for your thirteenth birthday?"

Aunt Cora wore a curious large locket round her neck, filled with elaborately plaited gold hair, with a matching ring. Amelia's eyes were drawn to it.

"Aunt Cora…I was wondering. About my birthday …well… that is, my inheritance. My mother's travelling chest…the Marchmont Chest. Every girl in my family, when she turns thirteen…"

"Yes, my dear husband did mention it. So exciting. Most mysterious. Probably not of much monetary value in it I imagine, though."

"Well I thought…I mean, I think it may contain some quite valuable things. My parents always said..."

Her aunt interrupted, "We'll all go to the lawyer together. Mr. Jerome Haverstock. Then we can have fun unpacking its little treasures together. There might be some pretty things for your room. Or a jewel we could have re-set. Run along now and change for dinner."

Aunt Cora held out her arms to be kissed and Amelia forced herself to enter the tight, perfumed embrace. Her aunt's cheek felt chalky with powder. Amelia thought she might go mad with suffocation - like a cat that doesn't want to be held.

She wanted to kick this tightly coiled woman in her silken shins and run out into the Crescent and over Regent's Park and keep on running and running till she reached the Thames. Father. *"Missing-feared-drowned does not mean dead."* She'd find him, rescue him, even if it meant swimming to the Indian Ocean. He was alive somewhere. She knew it.

She stood rigid in Aunt Cora's embrace. It felt greedy, almost as though Amelia were a new possession.

"At least she is kind", Amelia told herself and this was a pleasant house in London. Not a crumbling castle, with a demented owner, like the gothic stories she and the girls had read after lights-out in the dormitory, thrilling to the plights of the pale heroines of The Mystery of Udolpho.

And she wouldn't be here forever. When the Marchmont Chest was hers, she'd have her independence. Her birthday was only a few days away. Then she could pay to go back to school. She wouldn't have to stay here much longer and, in time, her father would be found, *"Missing-feared-drowned, does not mean dead."*

Aunt Cora released her at last.

"I'll send Effie up to help you unpack," she said. "She's a little rough around the edges. I thought you could have her as a sort of lady's maid. Don't let her be over-familiar. You need to let servants know who's in command. Otherwise they feel confused - like puppies."

Amelia felt suddenly sick in the stifling room.

"And do ask Effie to let down your hair and brush it out before dinner. I can't wait to see it!"

Amelia was released, at last, from the hot parlour into the cool of the hall. She longed to run outside into the Crescent, to feel the air on her face. But, standing in the shadows was her Uncle. He seemed to be observing her. He was so unlike her father. Waxen-faced, joyless. A shiver travelled down her spine - a sensation which made her want to stand up straighter and sink into the wall-paper at the same time.

Uncle Enoch nodded curtly, then turned away to consult his pocket watch and start winding a tall clock that stood on the black and white tiled floor.

Effie

Effie, the apple-faced girl, led Amelia up to her new room on the third floor. Her legs felt cramped with the anger and pain of the day and waves of nausea coursed through her as she climbed the stairs.

"Well, this is it, Miss."

The room had been newly papered with a pattern of yellow roses and was rather pretty. On the chest of drawers was a stuffed fox under a glass dome. He had quite a sweet expression and Amelia decided to make a friend of him. She put Miss Lovington down next to him, and she let out her angry song.

"It's alright – we'll call him Herbert," she whispered to the bird.

She could feel Effie studying her with interest.

"Canary's pretty, in't she! All golden and stuck in a cage. Bit like you."

"I beg your pardon!" snapped Amelia.

"Sorry Miss, it just popped out. My ma says I talk too much."

Apple-faced. Grinning. Nosy.

"Let me help you unpack your stuff. Haven't got much 'ave yer! I heard you lost your father. Mine's crushed his legs and can't work no more and drinks too much gin."

"He's not dead. He just hasn't been found yet," Amelia interrupted.

"Ever been to the music hall, miss? My brother Fleet works at The Alhambra. The best music hall in London…it's in Leicester Square, in the West End…"

Effie did love to talk. She hardly stopped, in fact.

"He's an artiste, my brother. Got an act with his mate. There's the best songs 'n dances! It's like fairyland! Are you going to live here forever now, till they find you an husband?"

"Certainly not. I'm only twelve…well, nearly thirteen. I'll be going back to school soon."

Effie nodded, but she looked sceptical.

"Well, not that it's any of your business, but…in a couple of days time I'm going to receive my family inheritance. We're going to the lawyers to pick it up. Then I can go back to school and I can hire a detective to find my father."

Effie lowered her voice, "Be careful of the master, Miss. I know I shouldn't be saying this, and it's not proper, but... even the mistress, she's terrified of him. Sometimes he... He's got this walking cane..." she stopped abruptly, flushing.

Amelia wondered if she should be putting Effie in her place now but instead she said, "Show me one of these songs and dances, then."

Effie picked up her skirts and started to sing, clapping her hands at the end of each verse and banging her hand on her behind. Amelia laughed...for the first time since "before the gong".

"I thought you was going to be really stuck up and give me loads more work," said Effie breathlessly. "I'm downstairs and upstairs maid now and mistress' lady's maid and now your maid. Since they had to let the real parlourmaid go, on account of them not having so much money now...But you seem alright."

'Ha! Thanks very much," Amelia laughed again.

"S'alright."

"Well, how do I know if you're alright?" said Amelia.

Effie laughed and started singing again.

"He was a young soldier, as fair as could be, and she was an innkeeper's daughter….boom boom….Come on, Miss!"

Amelia stands up and joins in with the song, putting her hand on her waist, and jutting out her hip like Effie.

"She shouldn't have done what he wanted her to…"
Clap clap.

"Now turn, skip and slap your bum. Hey, you're quite good. You can't do it in a posh accent though – you've gotta sound cockney like me."

Amelia tried an Effie voice, "She shouldn't 'ave done what he taught 'er…Better?" laughed Amelia.

"Yeah much better! You still sound posh though!"

The door swung open and the girls froze, mid twirl.

"Effie Milk! What are you playing at? And, Miss Amelia, I don't think your Aunt would like to see you behaving like a guttersnipe."

It was the sour, whey-faced cook/housekeeper, Mrs. Dove.

"Effie, get yourself off down to the kitchen at once and help Clara with the puddings. You better be ready for the dinner gong, Miss Amelia."

Amelia sat at the dressing table and let her hair spring out of her school plaits. She ran her sticky fingers through the waves. Her face in the looking glass stared back, pinched and shadowed. Her eyes swam suddenly and she put her head up against Miss Lovington's bars. She fingered the gold locket round her neck - a birthday present from her father.

"Am I like you, Miss Lovington? At least you've got me. Who have I got?"

From the hall below a melancholy gong sounded for dinner.

Why should she take her hair down? she thought furiously, and plaited it up again.

Explorations

The next morning, after a lone breakfast of kippers and a leathery kidney, Amelia started to explore the house. Aunt Cora rose late, and her uncle was already out at his club.

Surely there must be some pictures of her father? As a child perhaps, with Enoch...Or of her grandmother Edith, whom she'd never met. Maybe she'd find some childhood letters or keepsakes.

She pushed open the door to Uncle Enoch's study gingerly. Several clocks ticked loudly. Uncle Enoch had told her at dinner that he wound and checked all the clocks throughout the house at regular times of day, "My household runs like clockwork," he'd said. It had sounded like a warning.

Polished mahogany chests lined the ox-blood walls. They were filled with displays of butterflies and moths: amber white, cloud grey - their lacy skirts pinned out like dead brides.

Tiny skulls, bleached white, floated in liquid. Stuffed creatures played out violent scenes under glass domes: a glassy-eyed owl held a struggling rat in its mouth; a mongoose and a snake were locked in an eternal battle, biting at each other's tails.

There was a ledger on the desk. She opened it. There were no letters, just unpaid bills from shops: upholsterers – two sofas; milliners - five summer hats; drapers - twenty pairs of lace gloves; florists - four dozen bouquets of roses.

There were no portraits or photographs at all in the room. Not even of Aunt Cora.

A case of shells neatly labelled – their fragile lips open and vulnerable… *"Chelinotus"…"Perna Ephippium – Etheria"…"Phalodymia Candida"*. They sounded like the names of imprisoned princesses.

Next to them a heavy, bronzed glinting conch shell looked like a tribal weapon, its whorls glinted in a mote of light in the vault-like room. Amelia put a finger out to touch one of its spines.

The clocks began to strike ten and the door creaked open. Amelia shrieked.

It was Effie, coming in to dust. Effie shrieked too.

She whispered anxiously, "Better not get caught in here, Miss."

Amelia nodded and crept out shivering; away from the cases of dead creatures.

Amelia received her instructions from Mrs. Dove, while Effie helped Aunt Cora prepare for her day. Her Aunt had spent the morning resting after her journey the day before and Amelia was to join her in the morning room.

Cora was lying on a sofa, dressed in a mauve, foamy day gown. She was picking at a dish of pink marshmallows and green peppermint creams.

"They're for my nervous digestion."

Amelia sat on a silk footstool by her aunt.

"Read to me Amelia, from the newspaper, or one of my quarterlies; but only items that are cheerful or maybe an exciting murder. Or a divorce. We are going to have so much fun! Tomorrow, when I'm rested, we'll start shopping for you. I'm preparing a list."

Amelia looked through the pile of illustrated magazines to find something to read from: "The Ladies Treasury"; "The Englishwoman's Domestic Magazine."

Amelia opened the "The Dressmakers' and Milliners' Gazette" at random. *"Heels should be about two inches high, as piled up hair adds a further five inches,"* she read aloud. *"...this season's shorter skirts may allow an occasional glimpse of ankle. That ankle must be well dressed."*

The morning room housed Aunt Cora's collection of porcelain shepherdesses. Dozens of them – simpering and pink-cheeked like sugared almonds.

"You shall look like one of my lovely china girls in the frock I am going to have made for you. With your hair in ribbons. Madame Victorine herself is coming to fit you the day after tomorrow. We must start a proper curling regime for your hair at night. And skin preparations for your complexion.

Amelia sighed.

"Let me look at you properly. Pull back the curtains and hold up your hands in the light, my sweet."

Amelia held her hands up, reluctantly, sweltering in the orchid-house atmosphere of the room.

"Oh dear. They are shockingly brown. All those rough outdoor pursuits at that school, I suppose. How do they think they're going to help girls find a husband like that?"

At last, Aunt Cora sent her to fetch a handkerchief and she could escape.

Amelia found the square of lilac silk, embroidered with shepherdesses, on her aunt's dressing table. It had to be doused in lavender water, so she tiptoed into her aunt's bathroom.

Through the open door into her uncle's dressing room she

glimpsed Uncle Enoch's cruel–looking, very modern copper mechanical shower bath. It had multiple jets of water, designed to hit various parts of the anatomy when a gentleman stood in its bronzed dome. The jets were labelled: *"Feet"*, *"thorax"*, *"abdomen"*, *"spinal column"*. Amelia shuddered.

Her aunt's violet-glass-fronted cabinet was full of medicines: kaolin and morphine; menthol and laudanum; sal volatile and cocaine. Amelia read the labels: Tinctures for *"grief"* and *"nervous complaints"*; *"feminine hysteria"* and *"episodes of the vapours"*. Effie had told her that doctors and healers and fortune-tellers came every week with new 'cures' for her sadness and ailments.

Coming out of the room with the handkerchief, Amelia noticed a door at the end of an unlit passageway. A purple velvet curtain had been half-pulled back, so that it was only partially concealing it. The hidden door was up a step at the end of the corridor, and she'd not noticed it on her other trips up and down the stairs.

The door to the concealed room slid quietly open and Amelia pulled back quickly into the doorway of her aunt's room.

Effie came out and glanced quickly around her, as though to check no one had seen her. She was carrying an armful of dead roses. She locked the door carefully and draped the curtain back, fully concealing it this time, and replaced the key in a hiding-place under a jardinière.

After dinner, as Amelia was reading in bed, Effie knocked on the door. Aunt Cora had sent her up with the beauty preparations.

"We've got to start improving your terrible hands and face, Miss. Mistress says they're 'horridly brown and rough from playing in the open air at school without parasols.'"

She was grinning.

Effie was to mix up the lotions in the kitchen and apply them to Amelia every night before bed.

Her face was cleansed with a lotion of witch hazel. Then a thick, white mixture of rosewater and egg yolk, beaten egg white and glycerine was applied, like a mask, over her face and neck.

Her hands had to be softened with a paste of porridge and lemon and something else, which stank fishily. She held her hands grumpily over a basin while Effie rubbed it in.

"Castor oil," said Effie cheerfully.

Effie could barely conceal a grin as a pair of shapeless muslin gloves, like mittens, were tied on to Amelia's hands over the sticky unguent.

"And then these go on every night before bed for you to sleep in."

"No. Not really! Ugh"

Effie tied the ribbons round her wrists. "And I'll have to take 'em off yer in the morning!"

Amelia spoke suddenly.

"Effie what's in that room behind the purple curtain?"

Effie flushed and nearly dropped the basin. She turned her face away.

"I don't know about any room miss."

Amelia watched her curiously, but felt her irritation rising. Effie seemed relieved to be able to stand behind Amelia as she started twisting her hair into dozens of tightly knotted curling rags, which stood up all over her head, so that her hair would fall into a mass of ringlets in the morning.

"You'll look like one of them shepherdesses in mistress' room after all this lot."

"You should mind your manners. You're a servant," snapped Amelia.

Effie's face clouded and her mouth formed a tight line.

"I'm sorry. I just…hate all this," said Amelia.

"I was just trying to make you laugh and cheer you up.
I'm sorry if I got above myself," said Effie haughtily.

"I'm sorry, Effie. This is…everything's new to me and…
all wrong."

Effie finished tying on the mittens.

"How am I to turn the pages of my book and put out my
candle?" wailed Amelia.

"Would you like me to stand here by you and turn the pages
for you, Miss?"

Amelia was just about to say yes when she realised that Effie
was joking, and blushed, "That will be all, Effie. Thank you,"
she said sharply.

"Good night Miss. Hope yer hands are nice and soft in the
morning and yer don't get an itch on yer head."

"Insolent", thought Amelia. "I should put her in her place."
She caught sight of herself in the mirror - a clownish, ghostly
rag doll wearing mittens and she laughed too.

Amelia was walking towards the purple curtain in the sickly moonlight. She started to draw it back to reveal the door to the locked room. The door was ajar, but when she pulled it open dozens of moths, large moths and butterflies flittered out at her, catching in her hair, struggling, beating themselves against her scalp. She shook her head to be free of them, plucking at their sticky wings. At last, she sat up in bed sweating, pulling at the tight twists of rags coiled in her hair. It was nearly dawn before she fell asleep again.

Shopping

As soon as Uncle Enoch had left the house the next morning, the whole household became filled with anticipation for the start of the big shopping day. Aunt Cora looked approvingly at Amelia's hands and her new cloud of golden curls.

"What an improvement already, darling girl."

Amelia rolled her eyes at Effie, who grinned. Aunt Cora was checking through a long list. She looked alive and vigorous.

"Gloves. Lots of lovely gloves to protect those hands from the horrid sun. One pair of daytime lace. Four pairs of cotton: pink, white, lemon. Evening gloves..."

Effie had been up for hours. She was Aunt Cora's lady's maid too, as well as being parlourmaid and helping Bitty the scullery maid. She got up at five every morning. After she'd got the kitchen range going and cleaned out the grates and laid new fires, she'd been in to undo Amelia's hair from the rags and take off the loathsome, sticky mittens.

Then she'd spent over two hours dressing Aunt Cora's hair into a high-plaited coronet with cascades of braided 'false hair'. Amelia had peeped into her room earlier and seen the hanks of human hair, attached to little combs, lined up on the edge of the dressing table like dead voles hung up on a farmer's fence. The elaborate coils were topped now with a tiny, violet hat.

Aunt Cora stepped outside with Amelia, a purposeful smile on her veiled face and into the waiting hansom cab that the hall-boy had whistled up for them.

"We are going to Oxford Street," she told Amelia. "We don't keep a carriage at the moment, I'm afraid. Enoch, in fact, often takes an omnibus and says he rather enjoys reading his newspaper upon it. Have you heard of the subterranean railway?"

"The Underground? Yes, a girl at school said she travelled on it."

"Terrifying," shuddered Aunt Cora. "I have nightmares about it. I would feel entombed alive, wouldn't you?"

A double-decker, horse-drawn omnibus hurtled past them, crammed with men. First-class sat comfortably on the lower deck and the second-class passengers clung onto the top. Advertisements on the sides announced a patent medicine for gallstones. Amelia wondered what gallstones were.

"I sometimes go to Whiteley's emporium in Bayswater," said Aunt Cora poring over her long list, "but I think, for your first essential things - Debenham and Freebody's on Oxford Street. Then Swan and Edgar for your stays and bodices. We must start giving you a more ladylike shape."

They snaked through the traffic – along Portland Place and Wigmore Street, towards Oxford Street. "Peter Robinson is a good drapers." Amelia sees Peter Robinson's new store on Regent Street, its whole window devoted to mourning clothes in violet and black.

"Oh this is going to be delightful! Just the two of us together like mama and daughter. I feel like a girl again. Never mind the extravagance!"

Amelia tried to smile. She supposed she should be grateful.

Aunt Cora leaned closer.

"We won't tell your uncle. Let this be our secret, shall we? Men never understand what a lady needs to do to be perfect. The countless things one needs just to stay fresh and pleasing and youthful and well-scented. Merely to keep up appearances, at even the most basic level, during The Season, is quite exhausting."

The cab dropped them in Regent Street. Aunt Cora started to walk towards the shining shopping emporium but was drawn to a group of shoppers gathered on the pavement around a makeshift table, covered in little boxes and glass vials.

A sign proclaimed:

"Doctor Wellgood's Scientific Elixir."

A red-faced man, doubtless Dr Wellgood himself, was holding up a bottle of black, viscous fluid.

"This, ladies and gentlemen, is what London fogs do to your blood. This black blood was taken from a lady after five years in our pea-soupers. My elixir purifies the blood in a fortnight. This," he said holding up another vial, "...is blood I extracted from that same lady after taking my elixir."

The other vial he held up was a pure rich red.

Aunt Cora seemed tempted by the elixir and started to open her purse, but the press of the crowd suddenly became too much for her. Amelia took her arm and steered her towards the grand glass doors of the department store.

Inside, Aunt Cora recovered her strength and navigated confidently. Goods were laid out in vivid profusion on mahogany tables and displayed in glass-fronted vitrines. Everything Amelia owned was "too plain" apparently. They examined painted parasols, fans, dancing slippers, hairbrushes, a vanity case, endless manicure tools.

From the haberdashery department they selected pearl buttons, lace trimmings and hair ribbons. A bolt of rose silk was ordered, after lengthy deliberation, from a rainbow of fabrics. And the finest white cotton lawn for her new undergarments and nightgowns. The material must arrive for the dressmaker Mademoiselle Victorine's visit tomorrow.

They whirled through a labyrinth of different departments. It seemed to Amelia like the Arabian Souks her father used to describe during their wonderful long tramps over Hampstead Heath. He used to make even a wet afternoon walk feel like an adventure.

Aunt Cora seemed full of energy and quite unlike her listless, sofa-self or the meek waif she became when Uncle Enoch was around. She ordered and commanded and priced things up.

Amelia wondered if the careful delivery times were strategically planned around Uncle Enoch's absence at his club. She began to worry about how much money Aunt Cora was spending on frivolous things: an embroidered Indian shawl and tiny mirror for Miss Lovington's cage, a pink glass toilette set, gold lace pincushions, a musical jewellery box with a tiny twirling hummingbird. But it all seemed to thrill Aunt Cora.

Cora talked of coordinating their outfits and hats. Amelia had a vision of them as two pretty figurines lined up on a knickknack shelf in a drawing room.

"I've had a wonderful idea. I think we might have the same dress made for us by Madame Victorine. Long for me and slightly shorter for you. Wouldn't that be delightful! We might wear them to an afternoon party together."

Amelia bit her lip, trying to remain polite. Cora was so thrilled with all the compliments the servile shops assistants paid her.

"You have such well-shaped feet and tiny hands - just like your mama's," the lady in "Gloves" said and Cora beamed with pride.

Amelia's scream vibrated inside her. She held it in and held it in, but at last it escaped as a rasping cry. "She is NOT my mother."

The whole department seemed to reverberate with quiet shock. A nearby customer raised her eyebrows and eyed them curiously. Assistants smiled politely or coughed, enjoying the drama that broke up their dull day. Aunt Cora looked mortified.

"My niece is tired. I think we both need a little sustenance."

She walked tight-lipped and dignified from the shop and Amelia followed, already slightly ashamed.

Standing outside, at last, on Regent Street, Amelia apologised for her outburst. Aunt Cora dabbed at her eyes with a lace handkerchief, avoiding Amelia's gaze and shook away the unpleasantness.

"One must always be so careful if you have beautiful hair and you wear it down. It can be…yes…cut off your head by child thieves with sharp shears. It's sold to ladies for false hair. Yours would fetch a large amount. The violent poor are all about us, you know."

Amelia looked about her. Regent Street seemed full of ordinary shoppers to her. No vicious urchins with shears in sight.

"Enoch says they will swarm us one day en masse. The mobs. There have been riots on the streets, you know. The little climbingboy who came to do the chimneys last month… I know he was selling information about ways to get into our house and, on The Crescent, Lady Ermine's Siamese cat, Sooty, was snatched for ransom. She had to pay four guineas to get her back."

"Well they must be desperately hungry," said Amelia. "Effie's father lost his job because he was injured at work and she has to send home all her wages for her little brothers and sisters. And they all work too, even the five year old."

"Well, goodness knows, that girl can talk. If she could work as hard as she could talk…but let's not think about horrid things. It's our duty as ladies to be as happy and beautiful and pleasant as we can. Always, no matter how we might feel underneath. Drink in the pain and put on a smile."

Aunt Cora adopted a sweet, forced expression. Amelia looked at her in disbelief.

"Oh Amelia. I am exhausted. Let's find a cab. Shall we go to the Aerated Bread Company and have tea and iced cakes? Sugar is so reviving. Let us celebrate our new pink frocks! Maybe we can find a shade of icing in the same colour."

She linked her arm through Amelia's. "Watch out for your hair! Feel awareness behind your head if anyone unsavoury comes near us."

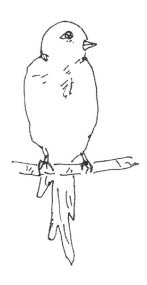

The pink dress

The next morning, after breakfast, Amelia glanced down the unlit passageway leading from her aunt's room. The purple velvet curtain was draped neatly in place. She started to tiptoe towards it. On the carpet at her feet she saw a dried rose petal and stooped to pick it up. Was it a clue? There was a creak on the stair. Uncle Enoch stood against the light from the window, a tall jagged silhouette. Amelia gasped.

"Are you lost, child?" his voice was infinitely cold.

"No, uncle."

How could he be her father's brother! They were so unlike. She curtseyed and ran down to join her aunt.

Amelia stood awkwardly on a footstool in her school undergarments, in the morning room. The bolt of pink silk from yesterday's spree was unfurled to exclamations of delight from Madame Victorine: a tightly-corseted, elaborately-dressed woman in jade silk, with a strange accent that Amelia was quite sure wasn't French.

She pinned a canvas pattern, which she called a "toile," onto Amelia. It felt very tight. Pearl buttons and lace were picked over from the department store treasure. There were endless discussions with Madame Victorine's simpering milliner

Mademoiselle Emmeline, about a matching lace hat. She had an even stranger French accent, which flowed freely in and out of cockney.

"Now. Is she too young to wear ostrich feathers if she still wears her hair down?" wondered Aunt Cora. "Not in Paris. Zat would be perfectly acceptable," stated Madame Victorine.

"Oh yez, parfaitly acceptable. In ze evenink," agreed Mademoiselle Emmeline, nodding her ribboned head emphatically.

Amelia stifled a yawn.

The pink dress was ordered for her birthday, as well as satin pantalettes, the feather hat, new nightgowns and a blue velvet cloak.

"Ze dress will be perfect for dancing, ve will leave ze hem short," trilled Madame Victorine. "My girls will work night and day on eet."

"I don't really dance", said Amelia.

A chorus of disapproving gasps.
"What on earth did that school teach you!" laughed Aunt Cora and Madame Victorine and Mademoiselle Emmeline joined in.

"Science, mathematics, Latin, algebra, composition… And French," said Amelia pointedly.

They all groaned. And may have flushed at the mention of the French. "So, nothing useful for real life. I don't think any of that is what a husband looks for in a wife!" laughed Aunt Cora.

Amelia, stared at the row of shepherdesses, letting their rosebud smiles blur in and out of sharpness. Her mind was elsewhere. All she could think about was how to get into the locked room and what on earth lay inside it.

Amelia sighed as Madame Victorine, Mademoiselle Emmeline and Aunt Cora discussed the important topics of the day: the merits of horsehair bustles for "obtaining the new shape of behind one needed to have now;" and the new cuirasse bodice featured in the latest "Dressmaker's and Milliner's Gazette", which "flattened the stomach so nicely though it left deep welts in the skin.".

A horsehair-stuffed bustle was finally decided upon for Amelia. Madame Victorine's assistant would teach her how to sit down in it when it was delivered.

It was Mr.s. Dove's afternoon off and her Uncle should be at his club. Today was her chance.

The locked room

Amelia waited impatiently till after lunch, a hash of last night's mutton and a sweet sago pudding. Aunt Cora retired to bed in the afternoon, putting on a satin eye-mask to sleep for three hours under the influence of various nerve-calming potions.

When all was quiet, Amelia tiptoed to the curtained doorway at the end of the passage, slid the key from under the plant pot and, holding her breath, slipped behind the purple velvet curtain and carefully slid the key into the lock of the hidden room.

The curtains were drawn on a milky twilight. Soft pink rugs underfoot. It was a nursery of some kind – a child's room, with papered starry walls, an ornate cot-bed with a row of animals and china dolls staring mournfully at her on top of a lacy coverlet. A tiny stuffed rabbit holding a dried pink rose was preserved on a pillow.

A nightdress case was elaborately embroidered with a flower-bordered name…. "ANGELICA." A painting of a perfect, flaxen ringletted little girl of about three years old. Rosebud mouth. Another painting of the same child with angel's wings.

And on a dressing table, laid out like an altar with candles and flowers, was a silver-framed photograph. The child was lying with her head on a pillow wearing an elaborate, white party dress. She looked peaceful; blissfully asleep, but Amelia knew she was not – she saw an edge of polished wood by the pillow. Amelia shuddered: The child was lying in its coffin. It was a photograph taken after death. A death portrait. Angelica.

Poor, poor Aunt Cora, thought Amelia with a rush of pity and understanding. No wonder she wanted to imagine all little girls were angels and ward away "bad things". She resolved to be kinder to her.

The cloying smell from dishes of rose petals was almost overwhelming.

Someone was coming.

Aunt Cora was calling out anxiously in the hallway, "Why is the curtain askew...and why…why is the door to her room open?" She peered in at the doorway in her purple dressing gown.

Amelia had crammed herself into a tiny wardrobe. It was full of elaborate little clothes. The rose petal smell caught in her throat with the fumes of mothballs.

Effie spoke from outside, flustered, "Oh I'm so sorry madam, please don't distress yourself. I must have left it open while I was changing the roses. I am so sorry."

"You thoughtless, silly, careless girl. Now all the benefit of my afternoon rest is quite undone."

"Yes madam, so sorry madam."

Amelia breathed again.

She waited a minute and then slipped out, replacing the key with a trembling hand. Effie led her mistress back into her dressing room.

Outside Aunt Cora's door she saw another row of perfect pink shepherdesses looking out. Effie shot a furious warning look over her shoulder at Amelia as she helped Cora into her foamy tea gown for the afternoon.

The swan girls

Amelia stood, toes turned out, in her new dancing pumps.
It was her first dancing class. Miss Frommerton, who spoke
in an affected trill, instructed Amelia how to dance a polka
and a waltz. She felt clumsy and flat-footed amongst the
other girls, a group of four sisters called the Swans: Cordelia,
Ephigenia and two identical, eerie twins who finished each
other's sentences, Maude and Agnes.

The Swan girls circled around Amelia with slanted smiles and
extravagant compliments, which veiled something. Amelia
knew they were trying to place her in some unknowable
hierarchy of their girls' world. Her serious education made
them wary of her cleverness and her orphaned state made her
pitiable, but also, somehow, romantic.

Afterwards, as they changed out of their dancing pumps.
(Amelia was grateful now that her aunt had bought her the
right sort from the department store) the Swans' mama said
she would send an invitation for Amelia to attend the Swans'
older sister, Gloriana's, party the following evening. It was to
be "a small ball."

Aunt Cora was delighted, talking as though she were a long-
suffering mama herself: Exclaiming at "how complicated
it was to have a daughter nowadays -organising her myriad
invitations and amusements and keeping up with her ever-
growing feet!" She fussed with Amelia's hair when a tendril
escaped from her tight chignon and Amelia, remembering the
locked room, forced a gentle smile.

In the late afternoon, after Aunt Cora's rest, Amelia sat
beside her wearing a pinafore, holding a tiny brush poised
over a china tea-set. She was trying to paint a design of Miss
Lovington staring mournfully at her reflection, perched on
a heart and snowdrops. Aunt Cora clearly thought it rather
peculiar.

"Fascinating, my sweet. Do you like mama's?"

Amelia nodded at her aunt's pastel confection.

"You are NOT my mama," she repeated inside her head, then
remembered she must be kind.

"It's very pretty. Might we visit the National Gallery one day,
Aunt?" she said agreeably.

"Well yes of course, my sweetest. Imagine that poor Violet
Swan – with five daughters to marry off…And the twins
are so unfortunately plain, poor things." Cora smiled
contentedly.

Aunt Cora trilled on about the elaborate cake for Amelia's
birthday tea in two days time. It was to be a pink castle, iced
with shepherdesses and tiny sheep. Every mention of her
birthday made her feel better. She would finally have the
Marchmont Chest and with it her freedom. She'd go back to
school and somehow initiate the search for her father.

That night, as Amelia climbed into bed, her hair in curling rags, face smeared with lotion, hands swathed in sticky gloves, in preparation for the ball the next evening, her head whirled. She didn't know what to make of her sad, strange discovery. Of the atmosphere in the house. Of the oddness of everything. So far, she had learned how to order a birthday cake, dance a waltz, embroider a kitten in cross-stitch, paint a teacup and had received an invitation to a ball.

The Lance would be horrified at the sickly artifice. And so would her father.

The Lance's voice reciting Ariel's song kept coming into her mind, *"Full fathom five thy father lies...those were pearls that were his eyes."* Amelia turned her rag-knotted head into the damp pillow and floated out to sea. But he wasn't under the sea. He wasn't asleep on a sea-bed, she knew it. She fluttered like a butterfly through the barnacled hulls of shipwrecks and he was nowhere there amongst the dead.

The swan ball

Gloriana Swan was eighteen and already "out". Amelia and the twins sat on a sofa watching her weave amongst the other older girls. Her dark hair was wound in snaky coils, entwined with lilacs; her feet darted in mauve satin dancing slippers.

The older girls waltzed past, charged with the serious business of attracting husbands. Their pink-white chests were almost bare, offered like cakes in their gauzy confections of dresses, whisking past in the arms of their black and white poker-backed partners. A blur of organza and tulle, citron and lavender: they sparkled brightly and talked about the weather.

Amelia sat amongst the young girls, their hair still curling freely down their backs, as they sat giggling on sofas. Were they wondering about when their own time would come – looking ahead with dread or sly anticipation? Eating strawberry ices in a cluster together was fun, but their coded conversations were treacherous and fraught with minefields.

How glad she was not to have to enter this race. As soon as she had her inheritance she'd no longer live in their brittle, artificial world. For now, she and Maude and Agnes Swan, too young to wear their hair up and dance with men, could laugh about the older girls' hunt for husbands.

Two girls fainted from their tight corsets and were dragged, quite roughly, to a small anteroom to recover on 'fainting sofas', where their mamas fanned them and pushed them back out again to lose no time in attracting the men.

Evidently you had to suffer and have an eighteen-inch waist to be a success in The Season. "But mama," moaned a horsey-looking girl in yellow silk taffeta, "I can barely breathe."

Amelia heard her mama reply acidly under her breath, "You know you might have only one more year before you lose your bloom, Griselda. Look at the Smeltings' girl, already on the shelf. You know how much papa has spent on you this year."

The mamas dabbed their daughters' wrists with cologne, mopped their sweaty palms, pinched their cheeks to give them colour and pushed them back out onto the dance-floor to greet the next partner on their dance-card and display their wares.

The plainer girls sat against the wall, trying to look dazzling and unconcerned that they didn't have partners, chatting brightly to one another, their eyes flitting anxiously to the dance-floor and back, where their prettier rivals twirled and sparkled. Amelia saw them glance anxiously at their dance cards, tied to their wrists with golden cords and teeny pencils.

If there were, "shaming white gaps in them…or even maybe no lines filled in at all, it means that partners haven't chosen them for dances," explained Maude Swan darkly. "Because they're too plain or too fat or too spotty or too poor. Gloriana worries that her nose is…"

"…too long - she sleeps with a clothes peg on it at night, to stop it growing," chimed in Agnes. "And Cordelia thinks her feet are too big. Those dancing slippers she's wearing are a size…"

"…too small and her toes are all crushed up and there'll be blood in them at the end of the ball…She squirts lemon juice on her bosom to make it whiter," chipped in Maude, finishing her sister's sentence.

The mothers, aunts and grandmothers sat, dressed in black bombazine, assessing the whirling girls' chances, snapping their fans open and closed like magpie beaks.

Amelia eyed Cordelia Swan, who was watching her older sister Gloriana, polkaing past, sparkling in the arms of a stout young man – her own hair coiled in dark masses too. Cordelia's neck was slightly longer than her sister's, her eyelashes thicker, chances brighter? She looked at Maude and Agnes, the two cleverer, plainer twins sitting beside her, gingery and freckled and fox-faced. What were their futures to be?

People swarmed urgently over to an elaborately-laid supper table at ten o'clock, as though starved: little birds jellied in aspic and towering blancmanges in rose and lavender were laid out amongst silver cake-stands ringed with delicate iced biscuits, cups of syllabubs and frosted bottles of champagne. Port-faced men forked mounds of roast beef and savouries onto their plates.

The girls in corsets could eat nothing at all. They sipped peach sorbets stoically from tiny iced spoons and eyed each other warily.

Amelia watched their tight smiles as they sucked their sorbet spoons, wondered if they worried they hadn't many hours left in which to shine…Later they would have their maids unlace their hateful corsets and lie in bed in their curl-papers, brooding on whether the night had been a success or not. Maybe their mamas would be angry with them, their papas disappointed. The money invested on a new dress for the ball: the carriage ordered, the hairdressers and corsages laid out for. Their third expensive London season and still no husband caught.

Amelia could see Aunt Cora's face shining, brittle with attention, amongst the other married and old women. She barely knew them, poor thing, and had no real friends. She was trying hard to fit in. What an odd, isolated, semi-invalid life she led on her sofa, with her peppermint creams and her shepherdesses, her lockets of woven hair, her terrifying husband and her sad, locked room. It was like living in a tomb.

In the carriage home, Aunt Cora was feverish and exhausted by the strain of having been at a party. It was after one o'clock by the time she had helped Effie prepare her aunt for bed.

Effie knocked on the door, bringing her a glass of milk. She took the hairbrush from Amelia who was sitting in front of her dressing table mirror and started brushing out her hair and curling it into rags.

"It's well after midnight so it must be Happy Birthday, Miss!" said Effie.

Amelia smiled, happy that she had remembered.

"Did you dance, miss? Was the supper good? How was the music?"

"They had little birds stuck in jelly."

"Ugh. Better watch out then, Miss Lovington." Effie squawked at the birdcage. Amelia laughed.

How different Effie's life is, thought Amelia. She knew Effie'd have to be up in four hours to start cleaning out the fireplaces. She wanted to hug her and tell her how stifling and awful it had all been. But surely it was a wonder compared to Effie's narrow, hard-working life?

Where would she, herself, fit into all this…the finery and husband-seeking, after she left school? Did she want the independence that Miss Lancer had? Where did a young woman, who didn't only want a husband, actually want to be? Her father had always told her she must learn as much as she ever could and only marry for love.

Surely the Marchmont Chest tomorrow and her return to school would bring her liberty? She prayed silently that it would. In any case, it was a link to her mother and her mother's mother and would be full of thrilling secrets. She wished she could share it with her father.

After Effie'd left the room Amelia saw that she had left her a little present on the bed: the words of the music- hall song, written out in big uncertain printing on the back of a playbill for The Alhambra, rolled up in a ribbon. It was probably her only hair ribbon – otherwise she must have spent half a week's wages on it.

She span towards sleep, with birds in aspic and mauve satin feet and the treacherous laughter of twin Swans, circling her head. She was thirteen. Happy birthday to me, she thought.

The marchmont chest

Amelia woke on the morning of her birthday to find a posy from Effie placed on her morning tea tray, which made her smile.

At breakfast with her Aunt and Uncle Enoch there was the pink dress, wrapped in a shiny parcel with the silver-backed hairbrush. Her uncle's frosty displeasure at these gifts – only a fraction of the extravagance of the shopping spree, if he only knew - was barely concealed. Aunt Cora twisted away from his gaze.

Amelia was impatient to go to the lawyers and, so it seemed, was Uncle Enoch. They must leave punctually at nine. He simmered as Cora fiddled with her violet veil and umbrella.

Uncle Enoch had planned a little surprise for their birthday journey to the lawyers. A nasty one. The hansom stopped at Euston Station and Aunt Cora became flustered, "Why has the fellow stopped, dear?"

Uncle Enoch smiled in his beard, "An amusement for the girl. We shall embrace progress, Cora."

The mouth of the subterranean railway station at Euston lay before them. The Underground.

Aunt Cora blanched, "But, Enoch. You know I cannot…"

"Nonsense Cora. Be modern. Show the girl some spirit. And we mustn't be extravagant unnecessarily, must we?"

The clothes...all the other purchases from the department stores. Amelia sickened at the thought of all the shopping he would find out about. Haddock-eyed, he watched his wife turn paler.

They descended the broad stone steps into the underground chill, Aunt Cora leaning on Amelia's arm. There were three windows with clerks behind them dispensing first, second or third class tickets. After a spiral staircase they reached the platform chamber, which filled suddenly with a dense fog as a train approached. It was fiery-eyed in the smoke.

Carriage doors were flung open, a whistle was blown and they climbed into a first class carriage. Doors were slammed shut and then they lurched forwards and plunged into the tunnel. Not into darkness, as Amelia had imagined, for there were green gas burners above where they sat and the compartment was quite comfortable with wide upholstered seats and carpeting.

Amelia imagined the press of twenty feet of earth above them: there was a thunderous noise in the smoke-filled tunnels, but she found it thrilling. She had seen the third class 'carriages' behind them though. They weren't carriages at all. The poor travelled in open wagons, standing up, like cattle, hurtling through the darkness of the tunnels in the fumy fog, holding rags over their mouths to stop from choking.

Another station, whistles shrieked again and young men jumped out carelessly before the train stopped, hurling open and slamming the doors.

There were gusty drafts if the windows were open, so the headachy fumes in the sealed compartment made Cora choke and hold her temples. She sat rigid, her silk handkerchief over her nose, not daring to show Enoch how terrified she was in the enclosed space. Amelia held her hand and felt angry for her.

They arrived at Farringdon Station and she helped her wilting Aunt to step down from the compartment. Enoch barely bothered to hide his tight, cold smile.

The meek, plump clerk, Mr. Wimble, at Haverstock and Callowby's ushered them into Mr. Haverstock's cluttered office. The room, filled with toppling piles of books and documents, couldn't have been more different to Uncle Enoch's orderly ox-blood study. Mr. Jerome Haverstock was kindly, and much younger than Amelia had pictured him. How was it that one never imagined something to be as it actually turned out?

As he explained the lineage of the Marchmont Chest, Amelia noticed that Uncle Enoch's palms were sweating. He kept discreetly drying them on his silk handkerchief. Mr. Haverstock observed Uncle Enoch shrewdly as he signed papers for his niece.

"The necklace which bears the key is to be given into the possession of the recipient of the Marchmont Chest and to be retained by her," explained Mr. Haverstock.

He handed the key to the chest on a tarnished, antique silver chain to Amelia and she put it round her neck, next to her locket, holding onto the key like a talisman. Her mother must have worn this round her own neck once. Uncle Enoch frowned. The chest was to be delivered that afternoon by the carter.

"May I see it?" asked Amelia eagerly.

Mr. Wimble and another clerk dragged the trunk in from an adjoining room. At last! She had imagined this moment since she was tiny. It was ancient – Amelia knew it was Tudor. It was made of what looked like painted greasy wood but was actually boiled leather, explained Mr. Haverstock.

"D'you know what's inside?" asked Amelia, thrilled, her heart pounding as she knelt down to open it.

"No. It's stipulated that only the recipient should open the Marchmont Chest. That she may use the contents as she thinks fit, sell things of course, if she's in need, but must add at least one keepsake before she passes it on, at her death, to her daughter or the nearest female in the family line." Mr. Haverstock spoke with a hint of warning in his measured voice as he saw Uncle Enoch get to his feet.

"She'll wait till she's at home," her Uncle ordered and Amelia got reluctantly to her feet.

As Uncle Enoch stepped into the street to hail a cab, Mr. Wimble ran after Amelia, with a handkerchief that wasn't hers. She noticed, flushing, that Mr. Haverstock's card was wrapped discreetly inside it.

"Mr. Haverstock says - should you ever 'be in need', Miss. You must not hesitate to ask. Wimble ever at your service, Miss."

Treasures

Uncle Enoch gave instructions that the chest was not to be opened until his return from town. It must be placed in his study, which must then be locked.

But when, after two hours of anxious expectation, the chest was at last delivered to Park Crescent, Amelia, Aunt Cora and Effie could not wait. They stood outside the study door after the carter and the hall-boy had dragged it in. Effie had been instructed to lock the door.

Amelia's hands went to the key at her neck. She crept towards the study door.

Aunt Cora shook. "No. We can't."

"It's mine and I'm going to. Effie, keep guard at the door."

She was trembling as she knelt in front of the ancient chest. She rested her hands reverently on its treacly surface.

"Just one quick look."

She fitted the silver key to the brass lock. It was stiff but turned with a pleasing creak and she heaved the lid up. As it opened, she inhaled its smell of leather and mothballs and a heavy sweet scent. A rush of the past. All those Marchmont girls and women: their hopes, dreams, losses, loves...all the sad and happy and odd and tender keepsakes.

A tattered, fungal, leather-bound journal was tucked on top: The first page was inscribed in elaborate quill script: *"The most secret and sacred journal of Matilda Marchmont."* Tied to it was a golden heart-shaped brooch. Amelia's fingers went to a Tudor chatelaine, then she picked out a little enamelled box containing a pearl-edged locket of a weeping eye with a sapphire as a teardrop. A tangle of mysterious treasures and curios: a diamond tiara, a stuffed puppy….She began unfurling a lace wedding-dress with long wreathes of veil in tissue which had become entangled with an invention of some kind...was it a gyroscope?…Her heart was thrumming with excitement.

The sound of the front door: Uncle Enoch's imperious knock. Amelia dropped the lid, hands shaking to lock it. She fumbled to put the key back round her neck and slipped out of the room before Effie, straightening her cap and apron, hurried to open the front door.

Amelia, running up the stairs to her room, heard her Uncle calling for ink and ledgers. "It must be sensibly inventoried and locked up for safe-keeping. The study door is to remain locked."

Then he called for the key. The key that was meant to hang always at Amelia's neck. Mrs. Dove came to her room and knocked. She glared at Mrs. Dove as she held out her hand for the key.

Amelia shook her head and clasped the key on its necklace.

"Your uncle has requested it."

Amelia shook her head again.

"No. It is mine."

Mr.s Dove looked at her in disbelief and marched downstairs.

She heard her uncle's steady footstep approaching on the stairs. Without knocking, he swung open the door. He stepped towards her, casting his dark shadow across the room. His face was implacable as he held out his hand for the key. Amelia looked into his glassy, grey eyes for a moment, challenging him and then, hands trembling with fury, took the chain from around her neck.

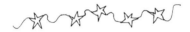

Effie came to Amelia's room later to help her dress for dinner. She flushed, faltered and then blurted out, "Miss, I've got to tell yer. I heard master saying to the mistress ...He says he's going to have the contents of your trunk valued and start selling things off. What was yours, was now rightfully his, as...your father's dead and you're under his roof and you belong to him."

Amelia felt bile rise up inside her throat. "I have to stop him, Effie. I have to do something. It's so wrong. Wronger than wrong..."

"But what can you do?"

Rage

Amelia walked down the stairs to dinner, white with anger.

After the soup had been served she forced herself to break the silence. Her voice sounded cracked and faint.

"Uncle. About my mother's trunk...my trunk…"

Uncle Enoch's face grew dark.

Her aunt began to shake.

"Amelia...I'm sure you don't want to make your papa angry," said Aunt Cora, imploringly.

Amelia stood up. Her spoon clattered noisily to the floor.

"Sit down and calm yourself, child," said Uncle Enoch quietly.

"I am not…I never will be...yours. I would rather die. How dare you steal my things! My…rightful, family things. I'm not your child."

"I said to calm yourself." His voice was steely.

'No. I will not calm myself. I'm not her doll. I'm not her dead child. I'm not an angel. I'm not her…I'm not… Angelica."

Cora shrieked and sank, in a faint, into a puddle of silk skirts. The housekeeper was called.

Uncle Enoch stood up, cold and furious. "Give me the key to the girl's room, Mrs. Dove."

Uncle Enoch grabbed Amelia by the wrist and pulled her out of the room, dragging her roughly up the flights of stairs. When they reached her room, he shoved her roughly backwards into it, so that she fell onto the floor.

"You will remain in this room until you have learnt respect and obedience. My brother was always a weak fool. He has produced a selfish, wilful child. Well, now he is dead, his duty falls to me. I will return in an hour to see if you have calmed. You will learn to call me papa, respectfully and gratefully. Or you may call me master, as the servants do. I will break your savage, female wilfulness and you shall be happier for it."

He locked the door from the outside.

An hour later Amelia heard his footstep, slow and heavy on the staircase. He unlocked the door and stepped into the room.

"Do you have an apology for me?"

Amelia made no answer. She held her mouth in a tight hard line. Uncle Enoch sat on the dressing table chair and brought a pamphlet out of his coat. He began to read: *"I never knew a vain, bold girl whose end in this world was not shame, poverty, or disease. For a time a bad young woman may seem to prosper; she may deck herself in silver and gold, she may paint her face like the wicked queen Jezebel. But these are the words of God, 'Hear thou this, thou that art given to pleasures, that dwellest carelessly, that sayest in thine heart, I am, and none else besides me; evil shall come upon thee, thou shalt not know from whence it rises; and desolation shall come upon thee…'"*

He looked up at the end of the page.

Amelia glared sullenly at him from the corner of her room.

"Am I your papa?"

She stared straight ahead.

"You shall call me papa. Or you shall call me master."

"I will not." Her face was white.

He stepped towards her and pulled her to her feet.

"Hold out your hand."

He pulled her by the wrist towards him and, taking a wooden ruler from his pocket, held it hovering over her hand, then brought it down, with a crack, on her palm.

Amelia had never been beaten. The shock of it filled her eyes but she stifled a cry.

"I will teach you gratitude and humility. You learnt nothing from my weak brother or his scandalous wife, with their ludicrous ideas about 'female education'. That school has poisoned you. You shall have nothing but bread and water and you shall not leave this room. I will come again and again until I see some change in you."

Amelia glared defiantly until the key had turned in the lock and then allowed herself to burst into furious, mortified tears. Her hand was already purpling with bruises and she could see the marks of measurements engraved in her palm.

A little later, Effie knocked gently and unlocked the door. She had a basin of dry bread and water on a tray and looked anxious.

"Don't be sorry for me. It makes it worse," said Amelia, turning her face away.

Effie pulled a bundle, wrapped in a tea cloth, from her apron pocket – a breast of roast chicken, a vanilla cake and some plums.

She noticed the bruise flowering on Amelia's hand.

"Wicked devil! Oh miss, I heard him say to mistress that he's going to sell all the valuable stuff in the chest. He only took yer in to get it and you are going to always stay as a servant companion to mistress Cora. She'll never let yer leave or go to school. And you know she's half barmy and wants you to be like the dead one to 'er."

Effie fetched ointment and a bandage for Amelia's hand and stroked her hair till she fell asleep at last.

She was so exhausted that she slept fitfully till morning. Father was dead. His eyes were pearls. How could he die and leave her here? The moths and butterflies flapped and skittered inside Amelia's head, beating themselves against her brain, trying to get out.

Prisoner

The next morning Uncle Enoch came again. He unlocked the door and pushed it open. He was carrying a folder of papers and an ebony walking-cane. It had a little fox's head in metal as a handle. He sat on the chair and read from the same tract as the night before.

When Amelia again refused to call him papa or master he stood up slowly and picked up the cane. The eyes of the fox on its top seemed to regard her for a moment. Coolly, he raised the cane over the photograph of her father and mother, brought it down, smashing it to tiny shards. Miss Lovington screeched.

"Turn around," he ordered.

Amelia screwed herself into a ball of pure white rage. The cane struck her on the back of her legs and her knees buckled under her. The pain was almost unbearable but she willed herself not to cry out. It would leave vicious red welts on her skin.

Light glinted off the fox's eyes as she collapsed back against the wall again.

Uncle Enoch threw the folder of papers down on the dressing table. Pages filled with names of shells written in tiny spidery letters next to faint illustrations, fanned out.

"You shall copy these annotations with perfect diligence and alphebatize them to demonstrate your humility. If you show carelessness and slovenliness, I will visit longer and longer lessons upon you."

As he unlocked the door Amelia caught a glimpse of Aunt Cora, standing red-eyed outside in the corridor. She saw that Amelia had seen her, averted her eyes guiltily and scurried away to the locked room behind the purple curtain. Now there were two locked rooms in the house.

It was after midnight. Amelia was lying in bed but couldn't sleep, her restless mind trying to seek a way to escape. The window was locked and too high to climb out of, even if she broke the pane. And where could she go? The creak of a stair made her sit bolt upright in bed.

Uncle Enoch was unlocking the door. He stood in the doorway with a lamp. He was holding the fox-head cane.

"Have you copied the annotations?"

Amelia clutched the eiderdown around her and pushed herself into the corner of the room.

"I have not."

"I see no sign of humility here. You disobey me in this one simple task. There may be a devil at work inside you. I have been too weak. Get out of bed."

He stepped towards her, grabbed her by the arms and pulled her off the bed.

He began to raise the cane. The fox eyes glinted. Amelia stepped backwards. Suddenly his face contorted into a scarlet twist of shock. Something heavy impacted into the back of his skull. He crumpled and collapsed onto the hearthrug. Effie.

Triumphant but shaking, Effie had clubbed him over the head with the bronzed conch shell from the study.

Uncle Enoch lay unconscious at the girls' feet, a mess of scarlet seeping from his head. Both girls froze as they stared down at his body.

Then Effie took a gulp of air, "Filthy beast. Well don't stand there gawping. Pull your dress on over your nightie and get that cloak on. Grab anything you've got that's worth anything."

Amelia scrabbled about the room.

"Miss Lovington!"

"Take the bloody bird, but hurry. I've given mistress a big dose of laudanum. She'll snore through for a while but Dove wakes easy, if she hasn't been at the sherry. Hurry up."

"Have you killed him?"

'Nah. Unfortunately. I think he'll recover. But I'll still hang if we don't get out of 'ere soon and they'll lock you up in prison or an insane asylum."

'But my trunk…he's locked it up…"

"We'll get it back somehow. I haven't worked it all out yet. I just wasn't gonna let him wallop you no more. Filthy pig. Just hurry."

"What about my wash bag… and my books." She snatched up the picture of her parents, smashed by Uncle Enoch, and Miss Lovington in her cage.

"Not much use for bathing where we're going miss, nor reading neither. Come on."

Amelia paused for a moment, stepped over the fox-head cane and spat in Uncle Enoch's unconscious, waxen face.

Amelia and Effie ran down the back stairs and out, through the area steps, into the cold night air of The Crescent. Clouds scudded over the moon.

"'Call me master' - filthy old madman," Effie panted as they crossed the street.

"But where on earth are we going to go now? All I've got is a shilling and my locket. Thank goodness I got Miss Lovington out!"

"Well, that's alright then! As long as we've got a non-talking bird that can sing three things that only you can understand. We'll make our fortunes! Blimey, we'll have to do some thinking now. I've lost my place and never get a character now. And if they come after me I'll be hanged and you'll be locked up."

Effie sank down on a doorstep, the dizzy rush of their violent escape leaving her now.

Amelia put her arm round her. "Oh Effie. I'm so sorry. Thank you. You did such a brave thing."

"Yeah well...Fleet'll know what to do. At least you'll never have to paint no more china again or do prancing with those stuck-up Swans."

"But where will we go?"

"S'alright. We can kip with me family at The Needle... in the Rookeries. Till we think of something"

"Maybe we could sell my hair."

Freaks

The girls walked from Regent's Park towards the West End with their bundles and the birdcage. Effie seemed quite excited now, as she led them over the lamp-lit streets towards Oxford Street, and down through Poland Street into Soho.

On the corner of Compton Street a gaudy crowd of young people, mostly women dressed up for a night out, were gathered outside a canvas booth set up by the back-room of a public house. Most of the men were off dogfighting or drinking, Effie said. The crowd pressed drunkenly – eager to take their turn inside the booth.

A boy of about fourteen, with a shock of dark hair, wearing a shiny, top hat and standing on a fruit crate painted gold, was announcing the delights to be found within. He spoke loudly in a bold, dramatic style, without seeming to draw breath.

"Step inside ladies and gents. Into the liveliest penny gaff in London, nay England, nay the whole of the western world. And you can be the first to say you have truly clapped your eyes on that most marvellous pairing...Leonora the Bearded Lady and Lusty Lusetta the Totally Tattooed Stunner...see them actually dance together. These two genuine, world-renowned, tragic freaks of nature. Step inside and see the stuff of dreams...the stuff of nightmares..."

Effie nudged Amelia. She was beaming proudly.

"That's 'im. That's Fleet!"

"Your brother?"

"Yep and we don't need to pay, nor queue. It's one of the best penny gaffs in London."

Amelia nodded, nervous but excited.

"Stay out of sight of his boss though. Old Hammerhead. He's fierce. And Fleet says his bite's even worse than 'is bark."

From inside the enticing, disconcerting canvas room, a golden light glimmered and flickered and a drum beat out an exotic rhythm. The sound of exclamations and shrieks and jeers rose up from its depths.

"Come on," Effie pulled Amelia deftly through the crowd towards the booth. Amelia heard a lot of swear words she could only guess at the meaning of.

Fleet looked her up and down and grinned as he parted the canvas and pushed them inside.

"Just room for these two young ladies, folks. Sorry ladies and gents, you'll be in the next showing..."

The tent was thrown into total darkness. The drum began to beat faster and faster, louder and louder, Amelia's heartbeat quickened.

"And now...let the show begin..."

Amelia had heard about freak shows – girls used to whisper about them in the dormitory at night. She'd always been secretly thrilled at the idea of them, but now she was actually standing in one, she felt a sort of sick dread. Her stomach was churning.

Effie gripped her hand as a flickering lamp lit up the makeshift stage – bathing it in a blood-red light.

"Prepare to behold," roared a thick-set older man, standing in front of a threadbare velvet curtain, "...the tattooed and defaced nakedness of Lusetta...complete in every inch of her plump flesh...adorned and engravened with ink, as she cavorts in front of you, shamelessly...with the tragically hirsute...that means hairy, ladies and gents...totally hairy... bearded damsel of darkest Borneo...Lady Leonora."

A few women giggled.

The man pulled away the velvet curtain and there, in a dim yellowish spot of light, stood a stout woman, stripped to the waist, tattooed all over with pictures of ships and mermaids and flags and hearts and stars. She turned round and, in her inked-over arms, was another even more extraordinary creature. Leonora was a foot taller than Lusetta, stubbly all over her body and with a thick beard, wearing a nightdress.

Her hands seemed almost like paws wearing rings. Her face was stubbled and thickly-bearded from her chin almost up to her sad, dark eyes. They were dancing clumsily, although it was hard to see in the dimly flickering lamplight. It looked as though she was wearing a small cage, like a dog's muzzle over her mouth. Was she so violent?

Music played from a barrel organ to accompany the women's strange, hopeless dance. The crowd oohed and aahed. Some jeered to cover their shock. Amelia felt thrilled and revolted and sad at the same time, as the pitiful creatures clomped and turned. Those poor, hideous women on display like that.

The stout man, evidently "Old Hammerhead," jumped on stage with them.

"Look at the accursed creatures", he roared. "They may dance, but would any one of you young men want to marry them, eh? Any of you young bucks brave enough to kiss Leonora, The Bearded Lady? Do you dare me to try?"

People in the crowd roared their assent.

Hammerhead crept towards Leonora and took her in his arms, stroking her stubbly shoulders.

"Ah, my beauty…come to me….Come to your Hammerhead."

Just as his lips moved towards her moustached, caged ones and the crowd roared and whooped, a great cry of anguish came up from Hammerhead.

The tattered velvet curtain came down and the lights went out and the crowd fell silent.

"Help me. She devours me. She is the very devil! She is the very death of me…" He screamed from out of the darkness.

The curtain was parted a slash - the red gas-light flickered briefly on again, to reveal flashes of the corpse of Mr. Hammerhead, lying blood-stained on the stage, his ripped-out heart lying, a livid, fatty, tubed mass on top of his bloody chest. Amelia felt faint.

The gas-light flickered off again and the crowd roared its applause and started to file out, well-satisfied.

Amelia didn't know what to make of it. She glanced sideways at Effie as they pushed their way out of the tent and the new crowd piled impatiently in.

"You look white as a sheet," said Effie. "You know it's all play-acting from Old Hammerhead, don't you Miss? You didn't think he was really actually killed, wiv his heart ripped out by the Bearded Lady did yer?" Effie was laughing at her.

"Fleet has to get that cow's heart off the butchers at Smithfields. It don't half stink after a few days!"

Amelia blushed angrily, "No of course not. I'm not stupid. I was just wondering what it feels like to be the Bearded Lady. She looks so sad and her life must be so strange. Does she speak English? "

Effie laughed again. "Well you could meet her if you like. Come on. Fleet'll introduce you before her next show."

Amelia looked horrified.

"Don't worry. She's not half as scary as me nan - wait till you meet 'er."

Fleet was having a quick smoke round the back of the tent. He cuffed Effie round the ear playfully and pinched her cheek, which she didn't much care for, so she kicked him, not so playfully, in the shins.

"This is my friend, Miss Amelia Elliot."

Fleet whistled, "Well you make a change from Bitty the scullery maid."

He looked her up and down from head to toe. Amelia felt a prickly uncomfortable blush run up and down her spine, in a most annoying and disconcerting way.

"Pleased to make your acquaintance, Miss Amelia Elliot," he said, with an ironic bow.

"She wants to meet Lady Leonora." Effie giggled again and Fleet winked at her.

"Well, I was just about to serve her meal. Why don't you join us, Miss Amelia Elliot? Not that Leonora is that used to genteel and polite society."

He took a last drag at his cheroot and led the two girls further into the narrow alley, towards another canvas construction. In the gloom, they passed the tattooed lady sitting on a crate in a dressing gown, drinking a mug of tea. Amelia nodded and said, "Good Evening". The woman laughed nastily and slopped the dregs of her tea on the cobbles.

"Mind yer manners in front of the quality, Lusetta," said Fleet.

As they walked further into the shadows Amelia could hear a low groaning sound and the clinking of a chain. Fleet picked up a plate of what looked like pigs' trotters. Raw ones.

"Follow close to me, Miss Amelia."

He spoke into the darkness, "Excuse me, Miss Leonora. I've brought a young lady guest to dine with you this evening."

Effie giggled. Amelia's heart beat faster. Her palms were starting to sweat. A high-pitched voice replied out of the shadows from the corner of the tent.

"Oh that's nice. Is she a smooth-one or is she a hairy-one like me? Is she a pretty?"

"Ooh she's glorious. Hair like spun gold. She looks like a smooth'un to me," answered Fleet.

Amelia flushed again. Vile, rude boy.

Effie pushed Amelia further towards the dark corner.

She could just make out Fleet. He was standing by what looked like a barred cage. Inside, crouched on all fours, in her white nightie, was Miss Leonora. She started to gobble up the raw pigs' feet.

"Say good evening to the young lady, Miss Leonora. Where's your manners?"

Amelia stepped forward, clearing her throat. Her knees were shaking. Why was the poor woman kept in a cage? Was she dangerous? Insane?

"Er...good evening. Pleased to make your acquaintance madam."

Effie pushed Amelia closer to the cage. The Bearded Lady looked up. Teeth, paws, bristly ears. Miss Leonora reared up on powerful hind legs in her cage. She was a bear. A miserable, shaven, chained-up bear. Amelia had seen one before dancing in the street near Swan and Edgar's department store. She blushed furiously.

Fleet and Effie exploded into guffaws of identical laughter. Effie imitated Amelia's high-pitched quivery voice, "So pleased to make your acquaintance Madam." Effie laughed so much, she doubled over as though she was going to wet herself.

Amelia ran out of the tent into the fog. The cold night air soothed her red face. Effie ran out after her.

"You horrible brutes. What a mean way to treat that poor creature. I hate you."

"Take a joke, Miss. You've gotta admit it was funny. Your face was a picture. Everyone thinks she's a woman. Not just you. You have to keep it secret," grinned Effie.

"I hate your stupid brother. I never want to see him again in my life."

"Really…?" Effie slipped her arm slyly through Amelia's. "So you won't want to be seeing him performing at The Alhambra then? And you wont want any of the succulent, steaming hot pie he's just give me a penny to buy…"

Amelia's stomach felt hollow. It had been a long time since Mrs. Dove's stolen milk and vanilla cake. And she'd never set foot inside a music hall. Much too vulgar for Uncle Enoch and Aunt Cora. She was desperate to go to one. She decided to swallow her pride.

"Well I suppose I must've seemed rather funny."

"Hilarious! You should've seen your…" snorted Effie, starting up laughing again.

"Just buy the pies, Effie," snapped Amelia.

The greasy, yellow pie from the pie-man's cart was fatty and thickly crusted with pastry, but Amelia thought it was possibly the most delicious thing she'd ever tasted. Eating in the street! What would The Lance, and the other mistresses at school, have thought! But then what would they have thought to see their pupil coming out of a penny gaff in Soho, with a sacked servant girl in danger of hanging, on her way to the rookeries, with nowhere to sleep and with only a shilling to her name. She felt a great welling-up of fear and self-pity and tried to squash it down.

They'd think it a bloody fine adventure, that's what - she tried to tell herself, in Effie's voice.

Amelia put her arm uncertainly through Effie's and they walked into the damp night, down the Charing Cross Road amongst the peacocks and dandies and Ladies of the Night, trying to look like bold Londoners and not a pair of homeless, penniless girls.

The rookery

A chill fog drifted over from the river. Clouds scudded across the weak moon. Amelia shivered and clasped Effie's hand tighter, as she pulled her towards the Rookery. Moonlight barely pierced the gloom inside the web of sordid alleyways that formed one of the most notorious slums of London.

Hungry, caved-in faces loomed out of the darkness. Crumpled skin like shrouds. Diseased mouths blabbering with drink or madness, hacked by coughs. Amelia set her chin bravely, though she didn't feel brave at all. But at least Effie knew where she was going, as she led them through the warren of paths and steps and makeshift bridges between hovels. She leapt surely over the little rivers of stinking human filth. Even this nightmarish place would be better than one more night under vile Uncle Enoch's roof, in that house of madness and pain.

"Nearly there, Miss," whispered Effie, pausing to catch her breath, "Look, there's The Needle." She helped Amelia balance, as they crossed a plank over a big open sewer.

Amelia had imagined The Needle would be a shining metal tower of some kind, but it seemed to be just one more higgledy-piggledy, half-rotten house with tiny, high, blackened windows.

They pushed their way into a narrow hallway. It was deathly cold, almost colder than outside, mushroomy with damp. Fungal flowers fingered over the peeling paper on the walls. Off the narrow hallway, Amelia glimpsed a long room crammed with about thirty or forty ragged men and women. It was lit only by two guttering candles.

"In there's the flophouse," said Effie.

The exhausted people, some of them sailors, were leaning against a thick rope down the middle of the room. They were sleeping or dozing or trying to sleep.

"They pay a farthing a night to sleep in there. There's only room to stand upright like that. You can't lie on the floor. If you can drink enough gin you can get yourself off." Amelia had never seen anything so frightful and miserable.

"It's better than being in The Spike," whispered Effie.

"What's The Spike?" Amelia whispered.

"The workhouse...the poorhouse. Land up in there and you're going round and round on the grain-grinding wheel for fourteen hours a day till you drop dead of exhaustion or consumption."

At the end of the hall was a kind of kitchen – thin, worn-out women huddled round a heated range stove, jiggling fretful red babies on their laps, wrapped in swaddles of rags and newspaper.

"That's where you can heat up your food. Meat and potato pies if you can afford 'em - from the pie-man in the street. Close your mouth Miss…Flies'll get in. Yes, it's not all satin shoes and ballet lessons for most people, you know."

A small girl, with violet eyes, wrapped in a holey grey blanket, looked up at Amelia as they walked past the kitchen. She opened her mouth in an anguished beseeching cry of hunger and toddled up to Amelia, feeling her crisp linen dress and velvet cloak in wonderment.

"Most of them kids only have one suit of clothes and one pair of boots to share between them. They have to share 'em out throughout the day, staying in till the next kid comes back home. They start working when they're four lots of 'em."

Amelia's eyes filled with tears, "I had no idea. I didn't know…" She took off her velvet cloak and held it out to the astonished little girl, but Effie snatched it back and tied it round Amelia's neck.

"Don't be so bloody soft. You've not got any more than them now. No room for pity any more. Come on."

Amelia felt sorry and revolted, at the same time, by the desperate creatures. Would she become like them? What really lay between her and them now?

"Don't worry," said Effie. "My parents've got a palace in comparison. They've got a whole room to themselves upstairs on the posh floor…well for them and me Nan and Molly and Tara and Henry and Little Pig. But I'm sure they'll be able to fit us in."

Effie led Amelia towards a splintered staircase. "Fleet sleeps at the artistes' gaff for The Alhambra now…the artistes' gaff is where the actors and artistes all live."

Amelia understood now what Effie losing her job meant for her family. Suddenly the gravity of it flooded over her. She and Fleet were the main breadwinners. They were the successes of the family, since her father's injury. Effie told her that all her little brothers and sisters worked, but they were too young to bring much money in.

"We'll just stay here for tonight and then tomorrow we'll come up wiv a plan to get back your trunk. Fleet'll help us."

Amelia felt light-headed with exhaustion. She was so tired as they climbed the rickety staircase, up to the fourth floor of The Needle that she barely mustered the energy to shriek as a rat ran over her foot.

Effie pushed open the door to be greeted by whoops of glee from a scrum of children who rushed up to hug her. A small fire burnt in the grate and the room was clean, and as well-arranged and tidy as it could be, with three adults and four children living and sleeping in it.

Mrs. Milk, Effie's mother, was a thin, pale, worn-out version of Effie – she looked old, even though she was probably much younger than Aunt Cora – so well preserved and primped and creamed. She had red sore hands from scrubbing and sewing the mail sacks that she worked on all day, as well as her ironing and laundering work.

Mrs. Milk drew Amelia kindly to the fireside while Effie poured out their whole sorry story. She moaned as Effie came to the part about bashing Uncle Enoch over the head with the statue, but the children cheered – thrilled by the story as though they were watching a play.

And Effie, warming to her audience, acted out the scene with gusto.

"Come here girl! Raise your nightie and bend over! I will flay the skin off your naked backside," she roared in Uncle Enoch's voice - exaggerating wildly, for dramatic effect. "... so Amelia was screamin' out 'No uncle, no, please don't beat me on me bare bum.' And then I cracked 'im over the head and he collapsed in a pool of blood."

The children were delighted and called for more details.

"How much blood was there?"

"Did he whack you first, Miss Amelia?"

"What was 'e gonna whack you wiv?"

Trying to hide her anxiety at Effie's newly-jobless state, Mr.s.. Milk offered Amelia a bowl of watery grey broth with a few pieces of carrot floating in it. Amelia knew she probably shouldn't take their precious food but she was so hungry.

"Don't give her our soup! What's she to us! Little la di dah china doll!" This was squawked out by a shrivelled figure, bundled in shawls, by the fire. Amelia hadn't noticed the morose old woman, her face wrinkled as a raisin in brandy.

"Give over, Nan. She's me mate," said Effie.

"Don't mind mother," whispered Mrs. Milk. "She's a cross we have to bear."

"I can hear you. A cross am I? Well don't you worry - I'll be up with the angels soon enough and you won't have to bear me no longer."

"If only!" murmured Mrs. Milk.

"Down with the devil, more like," sniggered a bright, dark-eyed boy with a runny nose. Henry. The old lady swiped at his neck with her stick.

"Cheer up everyone," said Effie. "Look what Effie's brought you all! Ta dah…"

With a grand gesture, Effie unfurled her apron and out tumbled a fall of shining Chelsea buns, fresh from Mrs. Dove's oven.

She'd swiped them on her way out of Uncle Enoch's over-stocked kitchen. Aunt Cora barely ate anything anyway.

"It's like Christmas morning when Effie comes!" The tiniest brother, Little Pig, shrieked with delight.

The children fell hungrily upon the glazed buns. Even the old grandmother cheered up a bit, as she sucked on a corner of bun with her toothless gums.

"Me 'n Amelia can bunk here, in wiv the kids for tonight, can't we ma, until we find somewhere else?"

The children jumped up and down excitedly on their bed, to show Amelia how fine and springy it was.

"Not another greedy nose breathing our air! There's precious little enough air for us. Little dollified creature," piped up the old grandmother. "And look! She's got a vast bird! We don't need a great animal breathing our air."

The children gathered round Miss Lovington in her cage.

"Oh, in't she dainty! Does she sing?"

"Why don't you teach her a few new songs? Rude as you like!" said Effie.

"Don't pay no attention to mother," whispered Mrs. Milk. "None of us do, me dear. And I've 'ad a lifetime of her. Of course you're welcome. You'll have to top 'n tail as best you can. "

"Yes you're welcome to as much air as you like and Henry's stinking feet," laughed Effie.

Effie dumped their bundles onto the bed they would share with Molly, Tara, Henry and Little Pig.

Amelia lay awake, shivering in the crowded bed, listening to a distant church bell chiming through the night hours. She could feel something biting at her ankles, which soon started to itch horribly. Her face was pressed up against Henry's left foot, his big toe poking through a hole in his stinking stocking, right by her nose. Nan's snoring mingled with drunken moans and a child's hacking cough from the room next door and sporadic whimpers from Little Pig.

Before dawn, Mrs. Milk was up, cleaning out the grate of the small fireplace with Effie. Amelia pulled her cloak round her and helped the children wash their faces, chipping a skin of ice off the top of a bowl of water. Effie broke a loaf of dry bread into a basin of milk for their breakfasts.

Molly and Tara wrapped themselves up in shawls. Effie told Amelia to hurry herself if they were going to be of any help.

"Come on, we need to get to Covent Garden before all the other girls get the best stock," urged Tara.

Henry and the four girls scurried out through the alleys of the Rookery. Other children, wrapped in shawls, many of them shoeless on the frosty pavements, were hurrying off to work too. Henry waved goodbye and turned off towards the Strand, where his 'patch' was.

"What does he do?" Amelia asked.

"He's a crossin' sweeper. Boys clear up the horse mess in the street so ladies can cross the road without getting it on their shoes and silk petticoats. You probably had 'em do it for you with the mistress and never noticed 'em, right?"

The air at Covent Garden was sour with the scent of fresh oranges and rotten cabbage and alive with a sharp sense of urgency and competition. Molly and Tara wove their way confidently through the throngs of dealers, porters carrying baskets of turnips on their heads and bartering costermongers. They passed other little tribes of girls – some waiting to buy watercress, oranges or flowers, like them. All were carefully clutching the pennies they'd made yesterday, to outlay today for the best-looking, cheapest stock. They'd be roaming the streets of the West End all day to sell their carefully arranged wares.

Amelia watched little Molly and Tara, younger than the Swan twins, haggling shrewdly with the tough, red-faced men for ferns, crysanthemums and gypsophilla.

They slipped into an alley and Effie started to help them sort and tie the flowers into little bunches for men's buttonholes.

Amelia's fingers felt huge and clumsy as Effie piled flowers onto her lap.

"We need to get to Charing Cross before the Smith girls," said Molly anxiously, glancing at Amelia's efforts and back at Effie. Amelia had crushed so many petals that Molly and Tara were terrified she was going to spoil their precious day's stock.

"D'you want to go to the station and sell buttonholes to businessmen or help me ma with her work at the Laundry?" asked Effie.

Effie spotted Mrs. Milk first, through the curtains of steam, hunched over a trough between two boiling vats of water. It was very hot in the Laundry and Amelia's legs were soaked up to the knee with the water that sloshed over the tiled floor out of the troughs. Her face and arms became drenched with steam and sweat after the cold of the streets.

Effie started helping her mother haul her pile of dirty shirts into the troughs of water. She scrubbed them with a cake of hard yellow soap and a bristle brush against a ridged board, like the other women. Amelia put her hands into a basin of water to reach for an edge of shirt and screamed. It was scalding hot and she pulled her hand out again, scarlet.

The women and girls, laundering around her, hooted with laughter. Like Mrs. Milk, they all had their skirts tucked up into their belts and wore soaked chemises and petticoats, their hair scraped back, their forearms and hands tough and red. Mrs. Milk whispered something to Effie and she pulled Amelia by the sleeve out of the steaming room.

Outside the Laundry, Amelia, soaking wet and now freezing again, sank onto a step.

"It's hopeless. I'm useless. What am I going to do?"

"You're not used to working, that's all and when we get your trunk back yer won't have to." Effie smiled at her. "But don't start blubbering. Alright?"

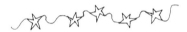

Amelia trudged wearily up the stairs at The Needle and Effie set them up by the small fire next to Nan and Little Pig, with the pieces of hessian that her mother sewed into sacks. Amelia could barely push the thick needle through the coarse material and kept losing her thread. It was so rough that her hands became sore after a few minutes and started to blister. It took her an hour to sew one ragged edge.

At least she could tell Little Pig a story. He listened intently as he played with his toy – a dog, called "Puppy", made out of sacking, with button eyes. Even Nan was listening. Amelia glanced up at her, thinking she might smile.

"What you call that!" jeered Nan at her efforts with the sack, "half-penny for twenty sacks…useless pampered little missy…using up our thread, using up our air, using up our heat…eating our food…"

Effie scowled at her and rolled her eyes at Amelia but Amelia could see nothing funny in it. She was useless and pampered.

By evening, when the children came home from work, and Effie was dishing out potato soup and spreading treacle on bread for their tea, Amelia was completely exhausted. She'd made one holey sack, which would have to be unpicked. Her hands were scalded and red raw and her ankles and hairline itchy with bites. She lay down on the bed.

"Come on," said Effie. "Get up. Comb yer hair. Pin on your smart hat. You and me is going up West. Fleet'll have an idea. He always does."

Amelia unwrapped her feathery lace bonnet. Molly gazed at it, fascinated, as she pinned it on. Effie pulled her out of the room, down the stairs of the Needle and back into the labyrinth of the Rookery.

Out of the warren of little alleyways they emerged onto the brightly-lit streets of The Strand and struck out along the lit up Charing Cross Road towards Leicester Square.

The Alhambra

The Alhambra was a vast, minareted place, like a Moorish
sultan's palace, on Leicester Square itself. Effie said Fleet
was near the bottom of the bill, but he could still get them
waved inside for free. Effie pointed out his name on the
posters in the alleyway near the stage door entrance.

Fleet and the Great Maestro Romano

"Who's the Great Maestro Romano? Is he Italian?"
Amelia asked.

"Nah it's Fleet's mate Rickie. It's a stage name. He 'n Fleet
used to be crossin' sweepers together before they got work in
the penny gaff. "

Effie started to push Amelia through the gauntlet of rough
people, who thronged outside the stage door. They were
shouting out at anyone who was allowed in through the
artistes' entrance.

"Are they waiting to see someone famous go in? D'you think
they think we're famous performers?" Amelia asked.

Effie laughed. "Nah! Fleet calls 'em Frillers. They're
threatening to boo off the acts that don't pay 'em to cheer
their bit. If an act gets booed a lot they get hooked right off
the stage, back into the wings and the audience throws rotten
stuff at 'em. It's horrible. Really funny. They stink when they
come off. Come on then...Look lively and smile sweetly...
we're nearly in."

Effie gave Fleet's name to the burly man on the door and he winked them in. Amelia followed Effie through the throng into the pit of the theatre, right at the front. So they were going to stand. It was a gin-soaked, shoving, sweaty crowd in the pit, but thrilling none the less.

The music hall was grand and beautiful and shimmered with chandelier light on velvet. Amelia had visited the theatre with her father once, for her tenth birthday, and sat in the dress circle on plush scarlet seats to see a Midsummer Night's Dream. It was the locket birthday. There had been real rabbits and trees on the stage and they had eaten violet and rose cream chocolates and held hands as she watched Titania the Fairy Queen through opera glasses.

She had felt almost painfully happy by her father's side and had wanted to crystallise the perfect moment in a glass case as though she could keep them both there, side by side, holding hands for ever. Like an exhibit in the South Kensington Museum. It would be labelled: *"Happiness: Elliot father and daughter."* It was as though she'd always known he'd be snatched from her one day.

The music-hall was just as grand and gilded and sparkling as the polite theatre: swagged with velvet and blazing with lights, but the audience was very different, even in the proper seats, not just the rough ones in the pit and the high-up Gods.

They'd come in after the interval and the lights dimmed and a sort of excited hush fell over the hall. Even the sweaty crowd in the pit.

The orchestra started to play an eerie melody on the violins and a top-hatted man announced in a booming affected voice:

"And now…the moment that you've all been waiting for. Madame Coralie Zarina: Reader of Souls. She who calls your Beloved Dead back from the Grave."

A single gas-light illuminated the scene. An agreeable shiver ran through the audience as a figure, swathed in white muslin, glided centre stage. She raised her arms – her face seemed almost waxen, with luminous skin and a scarlet slash of mouth. Her fingers waved sinuously in the air.

Madame Coralie began to sway rhythmically, as a drum- beat started up from the orchestra pit. Bathed in a green light, she murmured in a quivery, husky voice.

"Ahh…yes, now…my girls dance round me. My little guiding girls. Oh they're dancing…the little pretties. Do you have any visitants for us tonight, my sweet little pretties?"

Madame Coralie began to giggle in a tinkly, childish voice.

"Ooh yes. Someone's coming. He was limping when he lived on this side, but now he's running."

Bathed in the vivid green light, the vermilion tips of her nails fluttered about her temples.

The drum beat faster.

"Has anyone here lost a dear-one? Who used to walk with a limp?"

A woman sitting in the circle, wearing a ratty fox fur, stood up.

"It's my Father. Father dearest?"

A deep male voice issued from Madame Coralie's sea-green throat.

"Good girl. You always was a good girl. Peaceful here. All is peaceful and grand. I'm watching over you and the children."

'Oh. He means my sister's children, I suppose. Is Mother there with you, Pa?" She burst into happy tears.

"Yes, yes. All safely gathered in here, together. Farewell my daughters," muttered Madame Coralie's deep voice.

The woman in the fox fur wiped her eyes, "Goodbye dada. Goodbye." She nodded gratefully and sat down.

Hopeful, bristling expectancy rippled across the auditorium. The clairvoyant's eyes flickered and rolled back in their sockets till they were all whites. She giggled girlishly, taken over by the dancing guides again. Then her body became contorted in painful spasms. The giggles choked in her throat.

Amelia's heart began to beat faster. Might her own father be waiting to talk to her? Her legs felt weak. She could almost feel him close by.

Madame Coralie spoke, "A Beloved One wants to appear to her dear mother. A tiny, lost beloved one. Can she return?"

Amelia's heart sank.

"Do you have the strength, mother?" called out Madame Coralie. "She's only a small soul. A tiny revenant. But she wants to dance for her dear papa and mama."

"Flora!" Shrieked a woman in the audience. 'It's my Flora. Darling girl. Be seen! We're here Flora. Come to mama! We're here, darling!"

The woman's red-whiskered husband, in military uniform, put his arm round his wife, at once angry, embarrassed and hopeful.

The green light intensified. Madame Coralie opened her mouth, as if retching, and vomited out a plume of silvery smoke, shiny with fatty globules which formed into a cloudy miasma.

Out of the cloud stepped a spectral creature, about two feet tall, with a large head. It was wearing a white lace frock. Its features were indistinct but it was skipping around in a circle and clapping its little hands as though in delight. The drum beat faster.

"Flora!" screamed the woman in the stalls.

The dancing creature turned and waved.

Madame Coralie sucked up a great gasp of air and fell into a faint on the floor. The pale creature and her cloud disappeared as though snuffed out and the green light faded away.

The woman cried out again, "Flora! Come back!"

The audience was rapt. Motionless. The limelight flared up and the announcing man and a young stagehand rushed onto the stage with smelling salts to try and revive the unconscious Madame Coralie.

"Don't be alarmed, Ladies and Gentlemen. Madame Coralie is merely in a weak faint as a result of the spirit visitations."

The clairvoyant began to rouse, allowing herself to be raised gracefully to her feet by the stagehand. She leaned against him, looking uncertain as to where she was. The crowd bellowed its applause and she bowed modestly, as if she herself had done nothing.

"Thank you. They visit me. That is all. They visit me to show their love for you. I am weak now and must rest. Goodbye my friends. We shall meet again...*Be it in this life...or the next.*"

The audience droned enthusiastically along with her catchphrase - *"Be it in this life...or the next..."*

She was led, weakly majestic, from the stage.
Amelia's heart slowed again. No father. If only she could come again another night. Maybe then he would appear. He might tell her what to do.

"Wicked old charlatan," chuckled Effie beside her. "She puts on a good show, though, I'll give her that...and d'you know what...it's beginning to give me an idea that might solve all our problems..."

Amelia didn't have a chance to ask her what she meant, for at that moment, Mr. Wilkins announced the next performer: a woman in a baby blue pinafore with yellow ringlets, who bounced onto the stage.

'We present for your delectation...Missy Lizzie Dizzy! The Singing Schoolgirl."

Missy Lizzie Dizzy skipped up to him, sucking on a giant lollipop, and presented him with a stick of barley-sugar.

"That schoolgirl's forty, if she's a day," bellowed a stout woman next to the girls, who smelled of fish.

Missy Lizzie Dizzy started to lisp out a comic song, fluttering her false, yellow eyelashes.

"I've been kithed by tho many boys before," she crooned.

"Must've been pitch bloody dark then!" shouted another wag from the pit and the crowd roared with laughter.

"Tho many boys have loved me..." she continued bravely.

"Must've been in the blind asylum!" shouted out another wit.

More people in the crowd started jeering and booing. The first rotten tomato caught Missy Lizzie Dizzy square in the face, which brought more laughs and a cheer.

A chant started up from the pit.

"Hook! Hook! Hook! Hook!..."

Effie started to chant along with them and it spread to the stalls and the circle.

"Hook! Hook! Hook! Hook!," the audience bayed like wolves.

Missy Lizzie Dizzy faltered in her song. Panic spread over her painted face. Her eyes darted left and right. Suddenly, a large metal hook reached in from the wings and grabbed her round her plump, corseted waist.

A rancid egg and more tomatoes splattered on her chest as she was yanked, by the metal hook, off into the wings.

The audience roared its approval, enjoying themselves immensely now. They took swigs of beer and gin and bites of pie.

"How can she bear it?" said Amelia. "I would die of shame."
Effie was roaring with laughter and clapping and cheering.

"She puts 'erself up there in her paint 'n feathers. You gotta
be able to take it, if you want to put it about and have the
fame and the glory, dontcha?"

The lights dimmed again and Mr. Wilkins, the impresario,
roared.

"And now....all the way from sunny Italy, Maestros Romano
and Fleet bring their marvels of magic to the London stage."

Effie nudged Amelia in the ribs and urged her to cheer loudly
as Fleet and Rickie, both with shoe-polish-blackened hair,
curly false moustaches and scarlet waistcoats, leapt onto the
stage and into the limelight.

They started by jumping on and off each other's shoulders,
then produced teapots out of birdcages, from which they
poured themselves streams of feathers. All the while they kept
up a dizzying patter of spiky jokes. The audience loved them.

The performance was slick and sharp – one sleight of hand and
foot after another and it whirred through Amelia's brain like
a kaleidoscope. No threat of rotten eggs or the hook for Fleet.
Despite her anger with him, she had to admire his dazzle.

Then came a symbol clash, a drum-roll and the audience held
their breath, hushed and excited.

"And now, it is the time…" announced Fleet, climbing onto a chair, as Maestro Romano wheeled on stage a gleaming metal cabinet, shaped like a coffin. It had sinister-looking inscriptions and what looked like smears of dried bloodstains on the sides.

A drum-roll as Fleet intoned, "At last…what you've all been waiting for…the moment of truth…Who amongst you is brave enough to try it?…Who will sacrifice themselves?"

The audience started to chant, "Be-head the lady! Be-head the lady! Be-head the lady!"

Fleet opened the lid of the gleaming sarcophagus. Inside it was a sharp, heavy blade like a guillotine, but curved like a scimitar. It glinted in the sulphurous limelight and the audience shivered appreciatively.

"So now…who will we choose for our victim tonight? Who will sacrifice themselves to the great Egyptian Sun God Ramesesis?"

Fleet swung a light out onto the audience, lighting up the faces of women in the crowd, who shrieked excitedly.

"Which of you lovely ladies is brave enough to risk her pretty white neck? Who prays she won't *lose her head tonight?*"
"Who…," echoed the whipped-up audience at the well-known catchphrase…"Whoooo."

It was evidently the eagerly awaited climax of their act.

Amelia's eyes dazzled. The spotlight had fallen on her face.

"What's happening?" Amelia clung blindly to Effie in panic.

"Slice 'er head off! Slice 'er head off!" the crowd took up the chant all around her.

Meaty hands hoisted her into the air. Amelia shouted and screamed as she was passed roughly from man to man, up over the heads of the crowd, to the front of the pit and through the orchestra. The spot of light was still on her, blinding her. The audience was thrilled by her fear.

Romano stood above her, demonic in the footlights. He reached down and hauled Amelia up onto the stage and into the limelight, in front of the delighted, baying crowd.

Fleet walked round her.

"A real little princess, look! Golden ringlets and porcelain skin. What a gift this little white neck will be… if the gods choose to take it..."

Amelia stopped struggling. Her legs shook, but it was as though she was no longer in her body – the one that stood on stage, quivering in the limelight. Then she half-collapsed into Fleet's arms as he carried her over to the immense coffin-guillotine. This could not be happening.

"Off with 'er head! Off with 'er head", chanted the crowd.

Her heart thundered in her chest and she started to kick and struggle again in Fleet's arms.

He whispered into her ear, "Calm yourself down. Just curl up as you go into the hidden chamber. You'll feel it. It won't last long. Curl up small. Try and breathe slow."

The audience were on tip-toes as the terrified little girl, in her ladified dress, was pressed gently, but firmly, down into the appalling sarcophagus.

Effie, watching in the pit, turned pale. Even she was shocked at what Fleet had dared to do.

Romano spoke out in a grave voice, as a drum began to beat.

"Ladies and gentlemen, pray silence, so as not to cause our sacrificial princess further pain and distress…"

Amelia lay rigid in the open coffin, staring up at Fleet. Her head was clamped onto a scarlet pillow. She stopped struggling and prepared to die. Fleet whispered again as he arranged her curls beneath the shining blade of the guillotine.

"Crouch down into the second chamber after I've closed 'er up, spun yer and opened 'er up. Alright? Got it? Not till after I've opened yer up again. Right?"

Amelia nodded. What was he saying? She didn't understand.

Fleet slowly closed the coffin lid and she was in total
darkness. Where was the blade? Still hanging over the lid.

"Please let me die now," she prayed. Crimson slashes
flickered behind her eyelids.

Then she was spinning, spinning in total darkness and
silence. Spinning through an infinite night sky. Spinning
through the universe. Was this death, then?

Father beneath the black water. Guts twisting. Moth-wings
beat through her blood stream. Spinning stopped. Light
flashed onto her face again as the lid opened up. Fleet lifted
the top section of the sarcophagus. The audience saw the
pretty head lying on the pillow, face, a rictus of terror.

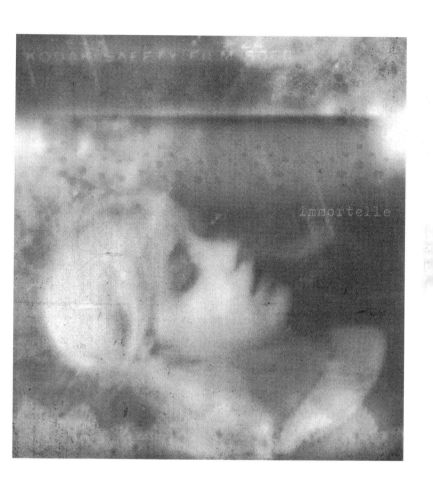

immortelle

"Bid our fair angel farewell, ladies and gentlemen. For, maybe, the last time on this earth."

The sharp blade hovered above her neck, glinting in the sulphurous limelight. Fleet lowered the coffin lid again with a sickening click.

Amongst the crowd in the pit, Effie held her breath. The bladed scimitar fell with a sickening swipe and there was a high-pitched shriek.

Silence and shock ran through the audience. The blade had sliced right through the coffin and glossy drops of blood trickled to the boards of the stage, beneath its neck.

Fleet gravely and ceremoniously span the sarcophagus again.

He spoke in the awed silence, "We offer this young angel up to you, oh Ramesesis. Will you take her?"

Ripples of horror coursed through the crowd.

"He's gone and done it. He's sliced her head right off."

One of the women in the pit fainted and was roused with gin. There were protesting shouts.

"Poor, pretty little fing." "Bring 'er back, you monsters!"

Fleet and Romano swung the closed coffin with its two sections – body and head. The two sections flew completely apart after the blade had sliced through them. Sad and grim-faced, they bowed low as they held the audience in the palm of their hands.

They brought the sections together, span the tomb again and then slowed it, bringing the spinning coffin containing Amelia's beheaded corpse, to a standstill. They prepared to open it.

"Let us pray, as we prepare to mourn the loss of our broken little angel," intoned Fleet. "Ladies and gentlemen...Those of a weak disposition, please look away if you fear the sight of blood."

The fish-smelling woman, next to Effie, was weeping.

"Now. Let us see - have we pleased the gods with our sacrifice?"

Inside the cramped lower chamber of the coffin, Amelia was coiled like a baby in a womb. She could barely breathe. Her knees pressed up into her chin. She span so fast that sour bile rose up into her throat and spumed onto her dress. She felt insane in the tiny space, her heart knocking hysterically against her ribcage. "Can't they hear it thundering through the wood?"

She could just hear Fleet, hissing urgently through the lid.

"Bring your head up and stretch out again. Quick. Do it. Now!"

Blood pounded in her spinning head as she uncurled and pushed upwards in the narrow box, out of the stifling compartment, as the top section opened out again and freed her shoulders. She stretched upwards till she was lying on her back again in the sealed coffin.

The spinning stopped and then light dazzled her eyes. Limelight. The lid was open. Night was gone.

The crowd roared its applause at the miracle of the golden-haired girl who had been put back together again, unscathed…

"Look. Her head has re-joined her alabaster neck unscarred. There is no headless corpse, ladies and gentlemen. The gods have spared her!"

Amelia was pillowslip-pale but intact.

Fleet and Romano lifted Amelia out of the coffin and set her on her feet. Breathing in tiny gasps, she could take in no air. Her legs buckled and she couldn't feel her feet. Each holding one of her elbows, the slick boys pulled her forwards into a bewildered, dizzy bow.

Roses landed at her feet. The crowd roared applause. Then, as suddenly, she was being lifted back down into the pit again and carried over the heads of the crowd, weaving her way towards Effie. She fell into her arms.

Fleet and Romano pranced off the stage triumphantly to a tumble of music and huge applause.

"That was a sight," grinned Effie.

Amelia opened her mouth to speak and vomited copiously all over Effie's only pair of boots.

Amelia's head was spinning as Effie pulled her away, through the crowd in the pit, and out through a side door. The doorman nodded them through and they climbed some narrow steps that led up to a warren of dressing rooms.

Amelia let Effie pull her along a corridor. They caught glimpses of artistes and acrobats, powdering themselves in bits of mirror, scrabbling over sticks of rouge and running through snatches of patter and song. The girls nearly tripped over two yapping dogs covered in spangles.

Effie pulled Amelia into a long low room where a tumble of ballet girls in sparkly tights and net skirts vied for space at the mirror. It smelt of sweat and candle fat and greasepaint, which the performers were daubing onto their clownish faces.

Effie elbowed a dancer off a battered old velveteen sofa, where she had been soaking her feet in a bucket of cloudy water, and sat Amelia down on it. The ballet girls gathered round the ashen quivering girl in their wide skirts, offering advice.

"Put her head between 'er knees!"

"Give 'er a nip of gin!"

'Try me smelling salts…one quick whiff."

"Unlace 'er stays!"

A tall red-headed girl, Greta, brought a cup of water, which Amelia sipped gratefully. Her mouth felt sour with sick and her insides were like cushion stuffing.

"I just want to go home."

And then she remembered. There wasn't any home. There wasn't even her yellow-papered room in Park Crescent. There wasn't her familiar, narrow bed in the dormitory at school. There was, for one more night, the infested mattress in the Rookery, shared with the Milk children, breathing the grandmother's begrudged air, her face up against Henry's feet. And then what? She felt her eyes fill up and proudly snuffed back tears.

Greta pushed her head down between her legs, thinking she

was going to faint again. Just at that moment, Fleet appeared. He bounded over with a huge grin on his painted face.

"Hello handsome," Nora giggled. "If you was a couple of years older…"

"Don't swell his head anymore than it is already," said Effie. "What you looking so pleased with yourself about? Look what you done to poor Miss Amelia. And look what she done to my boots, on account of it!" She pointed at her sick-stained leather toes.

Amelia's blood fizzed at the sight of Fleet and she tried to get up and flounce away, but she was so wobbly that the blood rushed from her head and she had to sit straight down again.

Fleet knelt in front of her, looking contrite.

"You were wonderful out there," he said gently. "You're a natural on stage, Miss Amelia. Did you see how the crowd loved you! So…if you play yer cards right…I might just have the answer to all your problems."

Amelia turned her head away coldly.

"I do not wish to talk to you. Please don't address me ever again."

Fleet turned to Effie.

"Mr. Erskine just nabbed me. He wants 'er to be part of

the act. On a trial obviously, at first. Says she's pure and innocent. Says we can try her out for a week. Paid trial. Well-paid trial."

"Go through that ordeal again! Never!" Amelia turned to Effie. "Tell your brother he is quite insane."

"Two bob a week and I could swing it for you and Effie to bed down in the artistes' rooming house. Be just you and Effie and one of the girls in a bed. Greek Street. Soho. All cosy and clean and a nice fire. And it's chops and mash on me tonight!"

Effie threw her arms round Fleet in delight.

"See I told yer Fleet would sort us out! The artistes' gaff. Not the Rookeries! Not Henry's stinky feet! Wages! Chops and mash. You'll be a famous stage artiste...and I can be your manager...or your dresser...or..."

"We'll find something for you to do too, Eff," laughed Fleet.

Effie pulled Amelia to her feet.

"So go on. Go and say thanks to Erskine, Miss Amelia. We'll come wiv you and we can negotiate your wages."

Greta and Nora catch on to the excitement too.

"Oh we'll be right cosy. We can show you girls the ropes. Look after yer. You'll be alright with us."

Amelia's heart clenched. She spoke in the most dignified voice she could muster.

"I shall never ever, ever do that again. I thought I was going to die. I thought I was getting my head chopped off. I was trapped inside a coffin with hundreds of people laughing at me. I would rather starve to death on the streets, or die in the workhouse."

Effie let out a huge sigh, "Well, that's bloody grateful! And that is exactly what will happen to you, if you don't take this chance…You will end up on the treadmill in The Spike. The streets of London aren't kind to a girl with no money and no family," said Effie sternly. "And what about me? I lost my place for you."

Fleet knelt down again and looked into Amelia's frightened eyes.

He spoke gently, "I know it was a bit of a shock and all of a sudden. But that's what a big theatrical moment is. It made the best dramatic effect like that. And they weren't laughing at you - they were marvelling at you! You were a complete wonder to them. You lit up their lives for a bit. Don't you like the thought of that? Just a little bit of you, deep down?"

Amelia turned away again but she was listening.

"They come to the halls…they're hungry, they're fed up, they've got their worries and you helped them to forget themselves and the drab world outside and all its horrors and pain. Well it's the best feeling in the world, I can tell you, to hold an audience like that in your hand. Like for those few golden moments nothing else matters. "

Amelia had to admit to a small tingle of excitement.

"Well, I suppose if I knew exactly what I'd be doing and it'd be planned and..."

"Yes, all properly rehearsed and worked out. You'd feel all properly prepared," Fleet agreed.
"Two bob a week, Amelia," said Effie excitedly, "And we can live together, with the theatricals. In Greek Street. We can buy pastries for breakfast. No more Mrs. Dove and Mistress…on at me from dawn to midnight…black-leading grates and scrubbing pans. No more nightly beatings for you."

"You might even get your name on the bill," said Nora.

"No, we mustn't let Uncle Enoch find out where we are," said Amelia, terrified. "But what about my trunk…I can't let him sell everything."

"I told you I've got an idea about that. Plenty of time to worry about it, tomorrow. Let's get a look at our new home," grinned Effie.

The artistes' gaff

A few hours later, Amelia and Effie were sitting, wrapped in shawls, in front of a cheerful fire, toasting hunks of bread and cheese on sticks, holding their chilled toes out to warm them.

They were in the dancers' room on the third floor of the artiste's rooming house, sitting on cushions. They'd been to pick up their bundles and Miss Lovington, from The Needle – promising to go back and visit the next day with some sherbet for the children – and they'd settled into the narrow Georgian house on Greek Street, over a baker's shop, in the middle of Soho.

The room was strewn with petticoats and boxes of face-powder and striped stockings and corsets and feathered hats. It smelt of cocoa and ballet-shoe-sweat and cheap scent, but it was clean and swept, warm and quite pretty and very cosy. The big bed had a patched, rose-coloured counterpane.

It reminded Amelia a bit of the school dormitory. She was used to sleeping in a room full of girls and it reminded her of a midnight feast adventure as she and Effie smiled at each other over their toasted cheese. They sipped a cup of sweet cocoa that Greta had made them in the kitchen downstairs, which she shared with the other artistes and their landlady.

The landlady was called The Duchess and she popped her head in to have a look at them. She'd been a great actress in her day, Greta told them. She wore a curled red wig and make-up, in the style of twenty years earlier, and spoke in a deep theatrical voice.

There were also a pair of haughty marmalade cats who matched the Duchess' wig colour. They were called Goneril and Ophelia. Amelia guessed they must be named after the Duchess's triumphant roles in King Lear and Hamlet. She explained this to Effie, who hated not knowing things, as the cats curled up on their laps. For once it was Amelia telling Effie something she didn't know.

Miss Lovington eyed Goneril and Ophelia with extreme suspicion as they nuzzled arrogantly at the girls' fingers for drips of hot cheese.

Effie was happy. She wiggled her toes to warm her chilblains. It was the nicest room she'd ever lived in. The one she'd shared with Bitty, the scullery-maid, back at Park Crescent, was up in the attic and had been broiling hot in summer and freezing in winter, with no coal for fires and bare splintery floor boards. Aunt Cora, with her pampered life on the sofa eating Turkish delight, knew nothing of the way her servants lived.

Amelia nestled comfortably into the cushions as yet another of the inhabitants of the gaff came in. Gertie was highly-rouged, but kindly-looking. She was a seamstress and ran up all the chorus dancers' costumes. She was an old friend of

The Duchess from her days of stage fame and shared a room upstairs with hundreds of the Duchess' old stage costumes. She asked Amelia to stand on a chair and gazed at her.

She opened up her sewing-box of feathers and glittery lace and held up a gorgeous piece of sky blue tulle.

She'd spoken to Mr. Erskine and he'd agreed Amelia needed a stage costume and that she should be the one to make it.

She lifted Amelia's skirts to look at her legs, which outraged Amelia, but Effie soon told her she'd better get used to it.

Gertie nodded approvingly, "Legs are a bit stumpy, but not too bad. Golden dancing shoes laced up to the knee, I think…Full short skirts with layers of tulle and satin. They'll fly out when you spin round…gauzy puffed sleeves…All gold and turquoise like the Egyptian antiquities at the British Museum…and a satin headdress with roses and gold edging that'll sparkle in the limelight…"

Gertie started snipping up a toile pattern and laying it against Amelia. Amelia sighed uncertainly but held up her arms, resigned. It was actually very exciting. Who'd have thought, a few days ago, when she was having the rose-bud dress fitted, that she'd be having a frock made by a theatrical costumier to wear on stage at the most famous music-hall in London.

"See, Miss. Them prancing classes with Miss Whatsit and them stuck-up Swans will have paid off," said Effie.

Amelia laughed and flopped down on the sofa, putting her head on Effie's shoulder.

"You know what I do like, Effie? We're equals now. So please, please stop calling me "Miss"."

Effie smiled. 'No we're not...not really. But don't worry, I'll stop yer every time you get too up yerself."

"Effie. I've got to get the chest back before he starts selling all my things," said Amelia, remembering herself after all the excitement.

Effie's idea

Effie and Amelia were lying in bed under the rose counterpane. Nora was snoring softly next to them, with her mouth slightly open. The sounds of early morning Soho, before the wintry dawn, drifted up from below. They could hear the bakers working in the shop, three floors down.

Amelia whispered in the moonlight that fell across the bed. The girls, though exhausted, were still too excited and lit up to sleep.

"When you get your first wages we might have another dress for Gertie to make, or borrow us from The Duchess," Effie announced mysteriously, "You know I said Madame Coralie had given me a brilliant idea...before you suddenly got up and threw yourself into the limelight, that is."

Amelia shoved Effie in the ribs, "Shut up. Not funny. Effie...Do you think the dead do come back? Do you think Madame Coralie could bring back my father? If he is...

Effie reached out and held Amelia's hand. She said gently, "The dead don't really come back, you know."

"But the lady's father. The little girl. How could she possibly?...We saw her there, dancing around."

"It's just what people want to believe. They want it to be true so much that it seems true. They want them to come so bad," said Effie softly.

She went on, "My ma went to a sitting with a gypsy once, who said she could see my little brother, what we buried when he was two years old. I could see the gypsy's daughter under the table, banging and sighing, but my ma wanted to believe it was Freddie...so I never told her."

Amelia looked at the cracks in the ceiling through a mist of tears, her hopes turning to ash.

Effie turned to her, "Madame Coralie's just a faker on a grander scale. I'll show you how she does it tomorrow. The little kid and everything. It's really clever but it's all tricks and showmanship. Smoke and mirrors, they call it."

"It doesn't mean the dead aren't with us though. Somewhere nearby," said Amelia.

"No, of course it doesn't."

"Because I do feel my father beside me sometimes. Urging me on," whispered Amelia.

"Of course you do. That's different. And you know what he'd urge you on to do...he'd urge you to get your trunk back. Not just for all the treasures but 'cos it's for family and for love. Your mother meant you to have it. And one day your daughter should have it and then her daughter. And I think I know how we can get it."

"We could never get back into the house. Uncle Enoch would have us both hanged or put me in a workhouse orphanage... and it's locked in his study."

"Not as ourselves we can't, no...we just have to persuade Madame Coralie of my idea. I didn't say it was going to be easy...it's going to be dangerous...very dangerous."

Effie's eyes shone as grey dawn light seeped round the edge of the curtains.

"Well, I'm going to risk getting my head chopped off by your crazy brother in front of hundreds of people every night, wearing a frilly skirt, showing my "stumpy" legs. What could be worse than that?"

Goneril and Ophelia jumped onto their bed, curving round their legs under the counterpane.

"Now. My idea. Them plays The Duchess did. Hamlet. What kind of olden day frocks did they wear?..."

Early morning sounds filtered upwards. Water sloshed out of buckets and was swept over the pavements as the Soho shopkeepers and costermongers started to lay out their goods.

Grimy frost flowers laced over the windows as Amelia looked down onto her new street.

The smell of fresh bread drifted up the stairs from the baker's shop and they hurried into their petticoats and underskirts in the chilly room.

Nora was still snoring as they quickly splashed their faces with cold water from the jug and used the chamber-pot behind the makeshift screen of a flower-patterned shawl.

Greek Street was coming to life in the milky dawn as the girls bought halfpenny currant buns, still warm, from the surly baker.

Then, arm in arm, licking the sugar off their fingers, they strode out through Soho, crossing Compton Street, towards Leicester Square, their frozen breath clouding their mouths. Even the sharp scent of rotted fruit and cloying flowers that the costermongers had brought from the last knockings of Covent Garden Market, smelt exciting to Amelia as their plan started to take shape.

Raggedy children had laid out pennies for the cheapest bunches of radishes or violets at the market to sell on the streets all day. One of the boys they passed was wearing ladies' buttoned boots with the toes cut out at the front and many of the girls were barefoot on the frosty pavements. Amelia saw that they were serious about their work. These were the kind of children that her Aunt had feared would chop her hair off.

But they were working at their trades: climbing boys and crossing-sweepers and flower-girls and acrobats. They were proud, not beggars. They were working to survive. Like her and Effie now, they had their place in the great, dirty machine of London.

Amelia thought of the girls at school sitting down to Latin or the girls in Miss Frommerton's dancing class, lining up meekly, toes pointed eagerly outwards, white organdie bows on their shining heads, dreaming of future husbands. Effie winked at a carrot-haired stall-holder's boy and he chucked them a couple of viciously green apples.

They were proper Londoners now, off to work.

Rehearsals

Amelia stood in the wings at The Alhambra with Effie. They were practicing catching the doves and rabbits that Fleet produced, and putting them back into their cages. The plan was that Amelia would be dragged on 'unwillingly' from the wings each performance, pretend to be terrified and surprised, and forced into the sarcophagus. Out of the limelight, the coffin looked much less terrifying – gaudily painted and crudely stuck together, but the guillotine blade was still properly sharp.

Fleet showed Amelia how to wriggle smoothly in and out of the sliding hidden compartment once he'd done the spinning. It still felt stiflingly cramped when she was crouched inside, but at least she knew she wouldn't actually be having her head cut off – unless she didn't get into her crouching position in time.

She made herself breathe regularly, as Fleet instructed her, and, when he spun the coffin round, the whirling darkness didn't feel so unknown and terrifying. This time she wasn't even sick.

She practised stretching upwards, lying flat and then getting out, looking dazed and wobbly like she had last night.

"You're a born performer you are," Fleet said as he pulled her forward to bow at the front of the stage.

Amelia laughed and tried to look as though she didn't care but she felt a strange melting feeling in her guts.

Effie said, "Even though I'm just catching the rabbits, I want to be on the bill – wiv a stage name. I fancy meself as Miss Ruby Clare."

Packing the props away afterwards in the wings, Effie nudged Amelia. Madame Coralie was on the stage with her assistant trying out a new effect. She barked out instructions in a broad cockney voice – not the exotic, wispy tones she'd used during her act.

A vile-smelling puff of purplish smoke erupted greasily from a contraption near the girls and a squat little figure jumped out, wheezing, from behind a black curtain. It was about three feet tall – the size of Little Pig. It had a yellow, waxy, sweaty face and waved its arms so that it could be seen reflected in a big mirror.

Amelia crept closer to the stumpy creature – curiosity overtaking her. Was it a child? It turned to leer at her – big head, small body. She gasped. It was a dwarf – he was older than Uncle Enoch.

"That's the child ghost," whispered Effie. "He's called Cedric. Look...the audience sees him in that mirror wiv the lace over it, so it's all faint and mysterious. And he appears just when the smoke puffs out of that thing. He wears sailor suits for boys, pulls on a nightgown for girls. Smoke and mirrors, see!"

Madame Coralie was satisfied with her new purple smoke and strode off the stage. Effie ran after her.

"Madame Coralie. Lovely effect, madam. I'm such an admirer of your work. We've, er, got a proposition for you..."

"What kind of proposition? Make it quick, I've got a headache size of bleedin' Essex."

The girls followed her as she swept into her private dressing-room and sat down on a leather sofa. Effie poured out her scheme. Madame Coralie should write to Aunt Cora saying she'd received a message that someone from the spirit world, someone passed-over, wanted to commune with her and fix an appointment for a séance. They knew Aunt Cora wouldn't be able to resist and that she would also carefully choose a time when Uncle Enoch would be out of the house.

That would be stage one. They could only hope that he hadn't yet sold the contents of the chest.

With the guarantee of the girls' first week's wages Madame Coralie was too tempted to refuse.

Amelia dictated the letter to Madame Coralie and they sent a boy to deliver it straight away to the house on Park Crescent. Next they spoke to Gertie. She willingly agreed to procure them a Tudor costume in Amelia's size.

A reply came back within the hour, to Madame Coralie's dressing room, with a meeting date fixed for the following afternoon.

The seance

Amelia felt strange but rather free as she faced herself in the mirror dressed in Fleet's old clothes, with her hair scraped up under a cap. Trousers and no corsets made you feel like you could run. Made you feel like you could do anything. Effie laughed when she saw her in her brother's clothes.

She wiped some coal-dust, from the grate, on Amelia's face.

"Too white and too clean," she said when Amelia protested.

That morning the girls had woken early, even though they'd been up late the night before, going over every detail of the plan. Their stomachs churned anxiously. What if Uncle Enoch was there? Amelia had to be completely unrecognisable.

Some spiced buns from the surly baker downstairs were sent up by The Duchess, to fortify them. Gertie, Greta and Norah hugged them and said "break a leg". Effie pulled a thick lace veil over her face. She was wearing a smart plaid dress from The Duchess' costume store and looked almost like a lady. Amelia pulled on Fleet's cloak over her second bulky layer of clothes.

Fleet roared with laughter when he came to pick them up.

"Nice clothes," he said to Amelia. "You look much better 'n me in 'em. Suits you being a boy. Bit fat though in't you?"

Amelia flushed, felt foolish and hot and scowled at him as she scrambled into the back of the cart that Romano had borrowed from a scene-shifter at The Alhambra.

Madame Coralie rang the bell of the tall house on Park Crescent and the door was opened by Mrs. Dove who ushered them inside. Amelia, slunk in behind her, with her head down, terrified that someone would recognise her. But no–one noticed the plainly dressed boy, in his deep-brimmed cap and rough cloak, next to Madame Coralie's eccentric magnificence.

She was wearing a purple bombazine gown with jet ornaments and a raven's wing hat. A real fox stole with a head and glass eyes, its mouth clasping its feet, was clipped round her throat. The fox reminded Amelia of the walking cane and a wave of good anger coursed through her.

Amelia remembered she was a performer herself now and decided to enjoy playing the part of a boy. She started to imitate Fleet's defensive, slick swagger.

Fleet nipped down the area steps to charm Bitty, the scullery maid, into giving him a cup of tea. Effie waited – heavily veiled, in the cart with Romano.

"Now. We shall need a room with dark curtains," said Madame Coralie, sweeping through the hall, sniffing the air. "The spirits and my guiding girls like darkness and peace. We are sure not to be disturbed?"
Mrs. Dove showed them into the parlour, where the thick

velvet curtains were drawn and the gaslight felt nocturnal. Madame Coralie walked about the room, "feeling its emanations" and called for the gas jets to be turned off and a single candle to be lit instead.

Aunt Cora looked nervous and febrile when she appeared. She seemed even thinner and frailer than ever. The clairvoyant spoke soothingly to Aunt Cora, "Sit opposite me, my dear, and close your eyes. Let me take your hand."

Aunt Cora was trembling, clearly swoony with her afternoon sedatives.

"You seem in some distress, my dear. Have there been violent scenes in the house? It feels full of trouble and secrets."

Aunt Cora nodded, coiled tight with anxiety. She spoke in little faint gusts.

"My husband has sworn me not to speak of…a distressing recent event. We had a visitor here in the house. Not the first visitor…the little visitor…the last visitor…Most perplexing and…painful. She had been poisoned…in her mind and she took a notion...and...she ran away. She…poor, silly, wicked girl...Everyone leaves me…every one goes…But it wasn't my fault."

Her eyes swam. She clutched at her throat.

"Well, maybe you will be brought some comforting message of guidance. From a passed one. They can give us direction in our lives, you know…Show us new paths," said Madame Coralie kindly.

They sat at the round table and she placed their clasped hands on its surface. Madame Coralie lifted up her head and then dropped it with a deep sigh. Her voice softened and deepened, "My pretties. Do you come to me? Are you dancing today, my dears, to guide us…Ah…a girl is coming…"

Amelia covered the candle and, in the complete darkness, slipped off her boy's cloak and trousers and pulled out full, pale grey velvet skirts. She shook free her hair under a veiled hood. She uncovered the candle again and let its flickering light fall on a puff of stage smoke.

In the tiny pool of light a spectral girl could just be seen in Tudor dress. She looked like Amelia, but she was transformed.

She spoke out in a clear, high, archaic voice, "I am Matilda Marchmont. Why have my keepsakes not been passed to my ancestress? You must do what is rightful…this woman will see that the chest is returned to my ancestress…if the Marchmont Chest is not restored…more pain will be visited upon your family. I, Matilda, shall not rest…"

Amelia was uncannily effective as her great great great grandmother. She stepped forward, raised her hand and pointed accusingly at her aunt. Then she smiled and blew out the candle.

Aunt Cora fainted.

In the darkness Amelia clambered back into her boy's clothes. They rang for the maid and Madame Coralie "woke" from her trance as smelling salts were brought and the gas jets lit.

Aunt Cora, pale and quaking, told Mrs. Dove to unlock the door to Uncle Enoch's study for Madame Coralie. Madame Coralie clasped Cora's hands, "You are doing the rightful thing, my dear. I shall see this returned to the girl. I shall find her. All shall be well."

She leaned on Bitty's arm and was taken to her room. She needed her vapours "tincture". Amelia felt a wave of sadness for her poor aunt, trapped with that dreadful man. Bitty gave Amelia a cautious, curious look as she passed.

They had to move quickly. She joined Fleet, who was darting up the back stairs from the kitchen. But when they were standing in the mahogany study, surrounded by Uncle Enoch's death collections - the bronze conch returned to its pedestal - Amelia froze.

"Don't think about him now. Concentrate," said Fleet.

In the corner stood the Marchmont Chest. Its lid open – objects ranged and labelled with numbers beside it on the desk, being inventoried and packed up for auction.

Amelia swept all the keepsakes she could see back into the chest: the eye brooch surrounded by pearls, the tiara, the golden heart. Fleet grinned at her as they closed the lid. Effie and Romano ran in to help and they heaved the chest from the room. Fleet grabbed her hand and pulled her from the house.

Madame Coralie stepped regally into her waiting hansom cab and disappeared into the afternoon. The sky had turned inky blue.

As they loaded the chest onto the cart Effie screamed: Pulling up at the kerb, in another hansom, was Uncle Enoch. Amelia's heart raced as he paid the cabman - still yet to glance up.

They piled into the cart and shouted at the driver to whip up the horse. But Uncle Enoch's waxen, still-bruised face changed colour. He had seen them and yelled at his driver to give chase. The driver whipped up his horse.

The twilight was already turning to night and a fog began to wreathe in. The roads were greasy with rain. It was almost dark and their horse, galloping too fast now, stumbled to avoid an oncoming omnibus. They weaved their way perilously in and out of the traffic coming from Great Portland Street, unable to see where they were going, but hearing Uncle Enoch's lighter cab gaining on them.

They swerved into a side street, trying to lose Uncle Enoch. Foley Place was dim in the fog, which was pooling about them now, thick as cream. They could barely see a yard

ahead or behind. Suddenly the narrow street was milling
with people: some kind of street protest, with men carrying
flaming torches. A flame spit, sulphurously and their horse
reared up, tipping them towards the crowd. Amelia screamed
- Uncle Enoch was fast behind them now. Through a sudden
eruption of flame, his cab lurched right into their cart,
splintering it under thundering hooves.

The noise of the collision was hideous. The horses wailed in
agony. The cart had caught fire from the torch-bearers' flares
in the fog. The mob Uncle Enoch had always feared was
trying to help the victims, but everyone was shouting and
confused, fighting the pall of blinding smoke and fog. Amelia
was trapped by her flaming cloak in the burning cart as Fleet
and Effie fought to drag her out. Her hair was a blaze of fire.
All scarlet. All black.

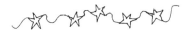

Awakening

Darkness. Whiteness. Red-veined dark. Spiralling down and then surfacing. A voice, a constant voice. Effie. Why doesn't Effie stop talking. Drowning in the night sky. Welcome blackness. Silence. Effie's voice.

Amelia wakes. She tries to open her eyes. A crust. There is something covering her eyes, not skin. She could see only milky-red light.

A hand takes hers. The familiar voice. Effie shouting, "She's awake. Master. Quickly."

Amelia's heart contracts. Uncle Enoch has caught them then.

"Why can't I see? Effie I can't see," she cries out.

"You've been asleep for so long. We thought you wos a cabbage."

"Why can't I see?"

She reaches her hands up to her face. It is bandaged all over. An unfamiliar sound: what is it? Effie is crying.

"They had to wrap up your face to heal it. Them. Your eyes. You've been asleep for so long. I thought you'd never wake up. The doctor's coming now, with the master."

"Uncle. But he'll kill us..."

"No Miss, not Mr. Elliot. We're at Mr. Haverstock's home. He's took us in. After the accident. I went to see 'im and told 'im everything. Don't over-excite yerself."

"Accident."

"The carriages crashed. The horses collapsed onto Mr. Elliot. He was killed. He was all burnt up. You was…well we thought you was going to be dead in the fire too, but you've been asleep for…more than three weeks now."

Amelia could barely breathe.

"They said if you woke up then they'd take off the wrappings…The doctor's coming now."

Effie held her hands tightly, "I'll be right beside you Amelia…"

Amelia's eyes filled with stinging salt. The bandages over her face were sodden. The room was milk. She touched her face and neck. Her hair was gone. Shorn short.

"They had to cut yer hair off, to get at yer wounds. But it'll grow back."

"I was going to sell it…Aunt Cora said the urchins…my head hurts."

"Shush," Effie soothed.

Effie jumped up. Amelia could hear her cross the room.

"Don't go Effie!" she screamed, but Effie was soon back and she could hear a trilling song.

"Miss Lovington!"

"Nora and Gertie brung 'er over and she's been singing to you to wake you up. Bloody bird, it's drove me mad. They and Greta have come to visit yer ever so often. And yer Aunt she came once…They let her out of the sanatorium to come…She went crazy after Mr. Elliot was took in the fire but now, she's more…well she's much more peaceful."

She gripped Amelia's hand again.

"Fleet's been every day to see if you've woken up. He pulled you out when you was on fire. Pulled your mother's trunk out too. Look, I put your key and your locket round your neck."

She guided Amelia's hand to touch the locket and the key.

"I heard you. I heard you from the bottom of the sea…talking to me.'

"Talking too much…it did come in useful in the end, didn't it?"

There were footsteps outside the door. A kind voice and then a hearty one. Mr. Haverstock and the doctor.

"Well, let's have a look at Sleeping Beauty."

Her pulse was felt. A cool hand on her forehead. She let herself be raised up on the pillows in Effie's strong, gentle arms. The doctor parted her bristling hair and fingered her skull.

"Healing nicely. Pain in your poor old head? Now let's take these dressings off your eyes and have a look. Try not to distress yourself. There may not be clear sight yet. Early days in a case like this. You're a very lucky young lady indeed to be alive."

Amelia didn't feel at all lucky, but said nothing as the gauze was slowly and painfully unwound from her aching head and face. Her eyes were free. She was almost too frightened to try to open her bruised lids. When she did there was nothing. No Effie. No doctor. No room. All was milk-white painful glare. She could see nothing at all. She turned her face to the pillow.

"Go away! Go away! All of you…Get out!" she screamed.

The doctor held her down and eased a sticky spoonful into her mouth.

"Good strong sedative. She'll sleep now, poor child. Poor little thing may never see again. Pretty little thing before, was she?"

Amelia drifted away. Golden coffin bed. Spinning, spinning again through the milk-white nothingness. Father in the dark sea. Pearls were his eyes. Fleet opening up the lid to heaven. At times, through the nothingness she heard Effie's voice.

Spoonfuls of broth and sharp elixirs put between her teeth. Miss Lovington singing.

Days later, she woke again.

"Effie, are you there? I'll not scream again. I understand."

'I'm here. I'm right here."

As Amelia turned her head towards Effie's voice there was a flickering at the edge of the whiteness. Like shadows behind muslin. A dark shape as Effie moved across the room.

"Effie. Effie. I can see it's you!"

Effie stayed by the bedside, excitedly clutching Amelia until the doctor arrived.

The doctor dabbed a stinging lotion on her eyelids, removing fresh crusts. Everything looked as though she was peering at it through the bottom of a thick bottle, and the light was searing – but she could see.

It was like a puppet shadow-show at first. There was Effie at the end of the bed now...and another shape was there – a boy's. A triangle of scarlet. A waistcoat? The shapes coalesced. They became more solid. Fleet. Fleet and Effie together.

She could. She could see them.

Fleet stood stiffly at the end of the bed. He smiled, shyly and seemed at a loss for words.

"Thank you," was all Amelia could manage to say.

She could see the Doctor's florid face looming over her.

"Well I am pleased. Very pleased indeed with you, young lady."

Amelia smiled at last, "Effie, I could murder a cup of tea!"

Sitting up in bed sipping at her cup of tea, she turned her head – a pink shepherdess with a sickly painted smile, floated vaporous by her bedside.

Amelia laughed, "Aunt Cora."

Effie nodded. "Never thought you'd be pleased to see one of them again, did yer! She came yesterday and held your hand while you was sleeping. Were sleeping. They're going to let her out of the sanatorium. Yer uncle was planning to lock her away in an insane asylum after he sold all your stuff. They found committal papers 'n everything. She's ever so much better and happier now."

Endings and beginnings

It was Christmas Eve. Amelia and Effie were sitting in
a window seat in the house in Hampstead, drinking tea
as snow fell on Church Row outside. Effie was reading
aloud dramatically from Matilda Marchmont's old journal,
which they'd found in the chest. Amelia could make out
the branches of the tall Christmas tree quite clearly now,
flickering with soft candlelight and hung with gingerbread
stars. The room was garlanded with ivy and mistletoe.

"Hmm. I've really taught you to read well," mused Amelia.

"Don't flatter yourself, will you!"

The girls grinned at each other.

Mr. Haverstock was walking across the room. His hands
were flapping oddly.

"Please don't over-excite yourself, but I have news.
Great news. More than news…A visitor. Can you bear a
tremendous shock, do you think?"

Amelia turned in the window seat. Her eyes adjusted from
the snow outside to the soft gloom of the room, slowly
picking out lines, filling in details, but she thought her
mind tricked her. Spots of light joined to make an indistinct
mosaic. The tall, thin figure of a man was coming towards
her. A slight limp. A dark, hopeful, lined face. Was it another
dream conjured up by the doctor's elixirs. A sweet dream

– for the shapes crystallized into a beloved, unmistakeably living person.

"Father!"

She was clasped in his arms. They clung to one another, trembling.

"Amelia. My dearest, bravest girl."

Mr. Haverstock had to help them piece the story together, for they could hardly speak for gazing and marvelling at each other. Her father had been discovered on an island, half-starved, dehydrated and his memory shattered. He was rescued by a Danish merchant ship and taken to a hospital in Copenhagen. His memory returned in sharp painful fits and jabs, in that peaceful place of clean- scrubbed white and grey. As soon as he could travel he began his journey to London.

So it was a very merry Christmas Eve supper in the tall house in Hampstead. Father, Mr. Haverstock, Effie, Aunt Cora, Fleet, Romano, Gertie, Nora and Mr. Wimble all gathered around the table to give thanks and to eat roast goose and plum pudding.

On Christmas Day, as the bells rang out, they visited the
Milk family in their new lodgings in Camden Town. Aunt
Cora was looking well and pretty, and blushed becomingly
when Mr. Haverstock shyly took her arm to guide her over
the frosty cobblestones.

They carried baskets of presents and sweetmeats for the
children. Mr. Milk had been found a new job by Mr.
Haverstock and things were better for them all now. Even
Nan didn't complain that the visitors were breathing their air.
Little Pig danced about in a smart scarlet waistcoat, stickily
kissing his new plush toy dog, his mouth crammed with
sugarplums.

In the coming week it was decided that, as soon as Amelia
was completely restored to health and sight, she would
go back to school, to board during the week and return to
her father in their new home, by Hampstead Heath, each
weekend. And Effie was to go with her.

It was a clear, crisp day in January. The day before they
were to leave for school. The two school trunks were nearly

packed. Effie was folding her new petticoat and school pinafore. As she closed the lid she looked up. Her eyes were full of tears.

"I can't go with you. I'd never fit in at that school. Despite how brilliantly quick and clever I am. I'm going to stay in the act. Fleet's nearly top of the bill now."

Amelia realised she wasn't surprised really. "But how can I go back without you, Effie?"

"We'll always be the closest of friends. Probably see you every weekend anyway. Me and Fleet. I mean Fleet and I. You'll soon be sick of us!"

Amelia sat in silence a moment and then took her birthday locket and put it round Effie's neck.

A new term

Amelia sat at her desk in a new classroom, next to Perdita Millbrace, on the first day of term. Miss Lancer addressed the rows of girls, all identical in their sober, blue-striped frocks and white pinafores.

"Welcome back girls. Today I should like you to begin by writing a three page composition. It will be entitled: *"What I did in the school holiday."* And girls...Do try and make it interesting."

Amelia's schoolmates' brows furrowed as excitements flickered through their heads – a skating party, a new cat, a day at the seaside.

Amelia smiled to herself and dipped her new pen in the inkwell.

THE END

Glossary

P5 Hall boy
The hall boy was the lowest paid, and probably the youngest, of the servants in a Victorian household. He'd work mostly in the servants' hall as well as doing lifting and carrying. In the Elliot household he would have cleaned all the boots and shoes too.

P7 Locket of woven hair
Victorians were very fond of elaborate 'mourning jewellery'. Rings, brooches and lockets were filled with intricately plaited hair from a loved one who had died. You can see wonderful examples of this jewellery in The Victoria and Albert Museum in London.

P12 Servants:
Lady's Maid
She would help her mistress to bathe, dress and look perfectly groomed. She'd look after her clothes, gloves, underwear and jewels and spend a lot of time on elaborate hair styling. It was a much more prestigious job than being a house or scullery maid.

Housemaid and Parlour maid
The housemaids did all the cleaning and dusting in the household. They'd get up very early to clean out the fireplaces and light the fires, and empty chamber pots. She'd also carry hot water upstairs for baths. The parlour maid cleaned and tidied the reception rooms – the hall, morning room, dining room, study and library. They might serve meals and afternoon tea and answered bells calling for service and the front door.

Effie did all the work of a housemaid, parlour maid and lady's maid.

Scullery Maid
She would carry out all the menial kitchen tasks, such as floor scrubbing and washing up. In the Elliot household, where there was no longer a laundry maid or kitchen maid, Bitty would have done the household's washing and basic food preparation for the cook, too.

P11 The Alhambra and Music Halls
The Alhambra, and its big rival The Empire, in Leicester Square in London's West End were two of the best-known music halls, though the city was dotted with music halls large and small. They were grandly decorated theatres where poor people, who couldn't afford the conventional theatre, could escape the drudgery of their daily lives and see dozens of different, often spectacular, variety acts a night. The successful acts became great celebrities of their day.

P15 The mongoose and snake
People in the late Victorian era were fascinated by taxidermy scenes, placed under glass domes. Animals of all sorts were stuffed, preserved and mounted for display. Often put into scenes that imitated nature, they look very gruesome to us today!

P19 Morphine, laudanum and cocaine
These dangerous and highly-addictive drugs were readily available in Victorian times from pharmacists to treat minor ailments such as headaches and stomach aches.

P19 Jardiniere
An ornate plant pot

P24 False hair
Women in the late nineteenth century would pay large amounts of money for coils of human hair attached to combs, for dressing into their elaborate hairstyles. This was sold to dealers by poor girls and women And the practice is still with us in the 21st century in the form of weaves and hair extensions!

P34 Horsehair bustle
A bustle was a large pad that built out the shape of a woman's bottom at the back of her dress. It became a very fashionable silhouette with a tiny corsetted waist, which had taken over from the crinoline (which gave an extremely wide-hipped look.) Bustles were often stiffened with horsehair. They were tied with tapes, over a woman's petticoat, around her waist and hips and under her bottom.

P34 Cuirasse bodice
This was a tightly-tied, long-waisted bodice, usually shaped with whale bones, that flattened the stomach and reached down to below the hips, which made it particularly uncomfortable.

P35 Sago pudding
A bland, economical dessert, rather like tapioca or rice pudding, made by boiling pearl sago with milk and sugar.

P40 Ariel's Song

From Shakespeare's play The Tempest.

P41 "Coming out"

One of the most important rituals in Queen Victoria's reign was the formal entrance into society of an upper class woman at the age of eighteen, called their "Coming Out." For the daughters of the aristocracy, the wealthy and the fashionable, this meant presentation at Court, a ball and a new wardrobe of clothes. It was very expensive for their families but a vital first step in the process of finding a husband. It was often marked, as Amelia notices, by a girl wearing her hair up.

P44 Blancmange

A dessert made with milk, cream and sugar and thickened with gelatin. It was often set into elaborate shapes and coloured pink or green.

P44 Syllabub

A luxurious dessert made with whipped cream sugar and white wine and often flavoured with lemon.

P62 Eiderdown

A duck down bed quilt.

P66 Freak shows and penny gaffs

Displays of unusual people, or animals made to appear like humans, in cheap shows or travelling fairs, were very popular in Victorian times. It seems barbaric and cruel to us today. "Lord" George Sanger, impressario of one of the

most famous travelling fairs of the period, talks in his book
"Seventy Years a Showman" of his many popular acts such
as: "The Smoking Oyster," "Miss Scott The Two Headed
Lady," and "Yorkshire Jack the Living Skeleton".

Wild animals such as bears could be easily bought, if you
had enough money. Jamrach's Wild Animal Emporium, on
Ratcliff Highway in London, even sold elephants and tigers!

P76 Rookeries
Slums or overcrowded living areas within towns, almost
like little villages themselves, were known in this period as
rookeries because people lived so tightly crammed together.
Thomas Beaumes in 1850 (see bibliography) describes the
rookery in Bermondsey: "Wooden galleries and sleeping
rooms…which overhang the dark flood of the river are built
in piles…little rickety bridges…span the ditches which
are the common sewer for drinking and washing water and
excrement."

P77 The Spike
A slang term for The Workhouse. For the very poor, the last
resort was to go to a workhouse or poorhouse, like the one
Dickens describes in his novel Oliver Twist. Families were
split up, given tiny food rations and worked long hours at
tough, repetitive jobs such as rock breaking, wood chopping
and corn grinding on a relentless human treadmill that Effie
refers to as "the wheel".

P84 Crossing sweepers
Like Henry, these were young boys who cleared horse manure off the streets when wealthy people wanted to cross over. Some of them would sell the dung - 'pure' as it was called - to tanning factories for use in leather making.

P84 Costermongers
They sold fruit and vegetables from barrows, in the street.

P97 Sarcophagus
In Ancient Egypt, a sarcophagus formed the outer layer of a body- shaped coffin, with several layers of coffins nested inside it, for a royal corpse which was embalmed and preserved as a mummy.

Bibliography

Primary sources
Thomas Beaumes, The Rookeries of London, 1850
Henry Mayhew, London Labour and the London Poor, 1861
Routledge's Popular Guide to London, 1873
G B Sowerby, Thysaurus Conchiliorum or Genera of
Shells 1840

Lee Jackson's Dictionary of Victorian London
website www.victorianlondon.org
contains a wealth of primary sources - extracts from
Victorian diaries, newspapers, memoirs, advertisements,
playbills, periodicals and maps.

Secondary sources
Peter Ackroyd, LONDON: The Biography, 2001
Kellow Chesney, The Victorian Underworld, 1991
Madeline Ginsburg, Victorian Dress in Photographs, 1988
Gilda O'Neill, The Good Old Days: Poverty, Crime and
Terror in Victorian London, 2006
Lisa Picard, Victorian London: The Life of a City, 2006
Peter Thornton, Authentic Décor: The Domestic Interior,
1620-1920, 1993

Thanks

Thanks to Frances Cain, big boss lady and mastermind
behind A Girl for All Time, for her commitment to publishing
intelligent stories for girls. To Rebecca Wolff who edited the
book. To Peter Salmi for his Amelia doodle drawings and
invaluable plotting advice. To photographer Nick Moore
for his photograph "Amelia's Butterfly Dream" and our
model Ellie Bligh. And to my son Raphael, who advised me
whenever he thought the story was "getting boring or sickly".

A special thank you to Louise Robinson for her inspiring
cover artwork and the illustrations "Immortelle" and
"Gossamer and Glass."

A Girl For All Time®

AMELIA, Your Victorian Girl™ is the second in the series of A GIRL FOR ALL TIME® dolls, novels and keepsake books. AMELIA's daughters' daughters will each tell their own thrilling stories from some of the most exciting periods in history.

MATILDA, Your Tudor Girl™ the first in the series, decreed that her travelling chest and its treasures be passed down to every first-born girl in her family to inherit on their thirteenth birthday.

You can read Matilda's adventures in MATILDA'S SECRET.

NORFOLK 1540

"Nothing exciting will ever happen to me"

Thirteen-year old Matilda Marchmont lives a dull life in the country – riding her horse, mixing her family's medicines, imagining herself to be a witch and writing in her secret diary. She longs for the glamour and thrills of life at court, led by her ultra-fashionable young cousin Katherine Howard.

And then one night something DOES happen. She is to be sent to court too, as lady-in-waiting and spy, to help further Katherine's marriage chances with King Henry VIII himself.

Matilda is drawn into a glittering world of intrigue, intense friendship and mortal danger which takes her from Hampton Court Palace to the Bloody Tower itself.

MATILDA'S KEEPSAKES
AND SECRETS BOOK

Your own customizable keepsake book: Plan a Tudor
themed sleepover with your friends, make delicious
Tudor treats, try Tudor vibed hair and fashion ideas, or
make your own family tree.

Re-imagine Matilda's world for yourself and your friends
and make a keepsake book you will treasure forever.

The next adventure in the A GIRL FOR ALL TIME® series features CLEMENTINE Your 1940s Girl™ in,

CLEMENTINE'S JOURNEY

Clementine Harper is 12 and attending Madame Pearl's stage school in Finchley when war breaks out in 1939. When the air raids start to hit London, she is evacuated to the country. Arriving in a tiny Devon village, clutching her gas mask and tap shoes, she's allocated to an eccentric widow's isolated house in frozen wintry woods. Clemmie is enchanted to meet another fish out of water, Giesella, a sophisticated Jewish girl, and they become soul mates immediately.

Giesella's family are still in hiding in Berlin in extreme danger. If only they could raise the money to help them escape…They decide to put on a show, bringing together other evacuees, people from the village and the eccentric Mrs. Milvaine . It's a shining sparkling, homegrown revue; a wonder amidst the darkness of wartime.

But will their plans to rescue Giesella's family succeed?

For more about your VICTORIAN GIRL doll, AMELIA, plus her outfits, porcelain tea-set and keepsake book, go to the A GIRL FOR ALL TIME website and find things to do, places to visit and recipes based on Amelia's story.

www.AGirlForAllTime.com

Note on the author

Sandra Goldbacher is a screenwriter and director.

She is twice BAFTA nominated, for her feature films:
The Governess, starring Minnie Driver, set in the 1850s
and Me Without You starring Michelle Williams, and Ballet
Shoes a BBC Christmas adaptation of the children's classic
by Noel Streatfeild, starring Emma Watson.

Most recently she has directed the opening episodes of
The Hour 2, a BBC2 drama set in 1950s London.

Sandra wrote MATILDA'S SECRET, the first in the series
of A Girl for all Time® novels. Sandra is endlessly drawn to
stories about the complicated interactions of young women.

Sandra lives in London with her husband and son.

21822693R20087

Made in the USA
Charleston, SC
31 August 2013